MYSTERY

COPY 46

J
Fiction St. George, Judith, 1931-
Mystery at St. Martin's / by Judith
St. George. -- New York : Putnam,
c1979.
    151 p.   cc 5-7

    SUMMARY: When counterfeit money be-
gins to circulate in her small New Jersey town and her father's parish seems
to be implicated, 12-year-old Ruth determines to help him by tracking down
the source of the money.
    ISBN 0-399-20702-3 : $7.95

    1. Counterfeits and counterfeiting--Fiction.
2. MYSTERY AND DETECTIVE 60661   N81
   STORIES
                                  79-17547
                                  MARC AC 4

(WEE) FICTION) ST

MYSTERY AT ST. MARTIN'S

MYSTERY AT ST. MARTIN'S

BY JUDITH ST. GEORGE

G.P. PUTNAM'S SONS • NEW YORK

Second Impression

Published simultaneously in
Canada by Academic Press Canada Limited, Toronto
(formerly Longman Canada Limited).
Printed in the United States of America.
Book design by Diane Stanley
Library of Congress Cataloging in Publication Data
St. George, Judith
   Mystery at St. Martin's.
   Summary: When counterfeit money begins to circulate"
in her small New Jersey town and her father's parish
seems to be implicated, 12-year-old Ruth determines to
help him by tracking down the source of the money.
   [1. Counterfeits and counterfeiting—Fiction.
2. Mystery and detective stories] I. Title.
PZ7.S142My [Fic]   79-17547
ISBN 0-399-20702-3

To my friends at lunch, with affection.

CONTENTS

MYSTERY AT
ST. MARTIN'S

·1·
ALL IN TENS

"TEN, TWENTY, THIRTY, FORTY, FIFTY, fifty-five, fifty-six, fifty-seven, fifty-eight, fifty-nine, sixty dollars. Dad, do you have a ten?"

"Mmm."

Dad was drinking his morning coffee and reading *The New York Times*, a combination that meant he hadn't heard me. Because he was dressed in a work shirt and his old gray sweat pants and boots, I figured it was either his day off, or he was going to saw up the tree that had fallen across the church parking lot. Since Dad's day off was Tuesday, and this was Wednesday, it must be that he planned to saw up the tree. Dad's outfit was scroungy, but even so, I liked it better than what he usually wore, a black shirt and round white collar. Dad was an Episcopal minister. It wasn't that I didn't think Dad was great, it was his job that got to me. Just because Dad was a minister, some people didn't think of us Saunders as being an ordinary family like everyone else, which was ridiculous because we were.

"Dad, do you have a ten dollar bill?" I asked again, louder this time.

"What do you need a ten for, Ruthie?" Mom asked. Mom was emptying the dishwasher and putting my school lunch together at the same time.

"I have to hand in my sixty dollar ski-trip money by October tenth and today's the ninth, and I want it all in tens." I had never skied and couldn't wait.

"Today is the tenth," Mom corrected me. "Henry, Ruthie needs a ten." Mom didn't raise her voice, but right away she got Dad's attention.

Because it was a dark, gloomy day that threatened rain, the overhead kitchen lights were on. When Dad looked up, the glare reflected off his bald head so that it shone like the apple Mom was polishing for my lunch. He smiled at me, and I smiled back. When Dad smiled, it was impossible not to smile too. Then he pulled out his wallet and handed me his last bill, though I was sure he hadn't heard why I needed it.

That was the kind of person Dad was, generous first of all, and second, vague. I was vague in the same way, only with me they called it irresponsible, they being Mom and my sister, Janice. Janice was twenty-five, a graduate student of biochemistry at Yale and getting married next month. I was twelve and in the seventh grade. Mom and Dad had wanted more children after Janice, but nothing happened. Then all of a sudden, there I was, their darling dividend. So, how come if I was the shining light of their old age, they cared whether or not I was brilliant like Janice?

"Ruth, are you coming?"

It was my friend, Phyllis Leggett, shouting from the front hall. I glanced at the kitchen clock. Seven forty-five! But I wasn't half ready.

"Here's your change, Dad. Thanks." When I handed Dad my five dollar bill and five ones, he looked puzzled, as if he'd already forgotten he'd given me the ten.

I ran past Phyllis and up the worn carpeted stairs into my room, threw on my sneakers, pulled the bedspread over my unmade bed, kicked my dirty laundry under it, tossed the wet towels over the shower stall, grabbed my social studies scrapbook, snatched my down vest off the floor, and tore downstairs, almost tripping over my old dog, Tippy, who was still limping up the stairs after me.

"There's the bus. Hurry." Phyllis slammed the door behind her.

I ran to the den desk and scooped up paste, scissors, and a Magic Marker. " 'Bye, love you," I called.

Dad always heard me say that. "Love you!" he replied.

"Have a good day, dear, and tuck in your blouse." That was Mom.

I stuffed my shirttails in my blue jeans. Mom always seemed to know when my shirttails were out, even when she couldn't see me.

Phyllis was already halfway down the block as I cut across our front lawn, my shoelaces flapping. The bus's red lights flashed as the cars began to line up on either side of it. Ernestine, our bus driver, planned her route with two extra minutes at our stop and that wasn't just for me. Ron Silver, next door, was even slower. I'd already reached the bus when Ron's front door flew open, and he raced down the street barefoot carrying his shoes and socks.

I flopped on the seat next to Phyllis and opened my scrapbook. Pictures, clippings, and labels scattered as

Ron jumped aboard, and Ernestine started up the bus with a wheezing grind of gears. I glanced out the bus window. Oh, no! There was Mom in her housecoat standing on our front porch in full view of everyone, waving the lunch bag I'd forgotten and looking really annoyed.

Gross! And I didn't have any money for the cafeteria, no money except my sixty dollars. "Did you bring your ski money, Phyllis? It's due today."

"I took in a check last week."

It was a dumb question. Phyllis never forgot anything. I patted the bills in my pocket to make sure they were safe.

"The day I took my money into the office that really cute Kenny Halberstrom was signing up for the trips," Phyllis commented. "You know who I mean, he's in eighth grade. I heard him say he's never skied before either."

I knew who Phyllis meant all right. I could have talked about Kenny Halberstrom all day. But I had to get my scrapbook finished. It was due first period, and Mr. Perly said he'd send a notice home if I got one more Incomplete. Incomplete seemed to be the story of my life. I wanted to be all together and efficient, but I never seemed to be able to pull it off.

My scrapbook was messy, but I couldn't help it. With the bus stopping and starting every thirty seconds, the papers kept sliding off my lap; and half the kids were smoking, which always made me carsick. Ernestine was a good driver, but she smoked herself so she didn't do anything about the kids. When I first started riding the bus in September, Mom accused me of smoking because my clothes always reeked of cigarettes.

"How're you doing on your raffle tickets for the Band trip, Ruth?"

Oh-oh, I'd forgotten them. That's how I was doing. Phyllis was really into Band and had asked me to sell raffle chances for their trip to Washington in January. She'd even written my name on every stub. And they were all still in my slicker pocket where I'd put them a week ago.

"Pretty good," I mumbled.

"Well, don't forget." Luckily Phyllis had something more important on her mind. "You know, I've finally decided what to do with my name."

"What?" I wanted to do something with my name too, but there wasn't much that could be done with Ruth Boyd Saunders. It was hard enough to get Mom and Dad to drop the Ruthie for Ruth, and forget the Baby altogether.

"I'm going to spell it 'Philys.' It sounds Greek, don't you think?" Our English class was studying Greek mythology. Phyllis probably pictured herself as one of those Greek goddesses. She was about a foot taller than anyone else in the seventh grade, and even wore a bra and got her period.

"Fantastic," I said, instantly jealous. It did sound Greek. Ruyth . . . Rudi . . . Rue. I'd tried everything, but nothing seemed to fit my round face and brown eyes, at least not the way Philys fit Phyllis's shiny blonde hair and long, thin legs. Since I had to put up with fair skin and freckles, it seemed only right I should have red hair. But I didn't. My long hair was straight and brown.

I was the last one off the bus. In fact, Ernestine waited while I pasted in my final clipping. Then I stopped at the office with my ski money which gave me another Tardy for homeroom.

The rest of the morning went as usual, until home ec. Sewing was my worst subject, and sure enough, right away I fouled up my bobbin. As I waited for help, I stared out the window at the eighth-grade gym class, running laps around the school. All of a sudden, Kenny Halberstrom sprinted past. He looked terrific in his gym shorts. Kenny was tall, taller even than Phyllis, and though he was thin, he was muscular. I craned my neck to see better. Wow, he even had hair on his legs.

I tried to fix my bobbin as I waited for him to run past again, but it was hopelessly tangled. It was especially maddening because the rest of the class was buzzing away like professionals.

The gym class rounded the corner. This time Kenny was third back from the lead, his long, hairy legs pumping. If only he'd look in our room . . .

"Ruth Saunders!" It was Mrs. Choy, our teacher. She was a tiny woman who could move sewing machines around like pencil sharpeners. She'd spotted me as a lost cause from the start, and we hadn't gotten along very well since.

I sat up straight with one hand on my machine, as if I knew what I was doing. "Yes, Mrs. Choy?"

"My dear child, are you asleep or in a trance? The office is paging your name over the loudspeaker."

I suddenly realized the room was deadly quiet. No one was running their machines or even talking. I blushed red as I stood up. Lately, when anyone looked at me cross-eyed, I blushed. I hated it, but I couldn't seem to control it. Still blushing, I waited for Mrs. Choy to make out my hall pass. Mom must have brought my lunch to the school office, which was surprising. Mom usually used things like that to teach me a sense of responsibility. Maybe Dad had dropped it off.

I walked down the green, carpeted hallway without making a sound. Outside in the courtyard, I could see it had started to drizzle. The weather was what I liked least about New Jersey. I had steamed like a lobster all summer, now it had rained almost the whole fall. We had moved to Fordwick, New Jersey from Walkerton in northern California last February, when Dad was asked to be rector of St. Martin's. I had finished up sixth grade at the grade school down the block, then in September, started seventh grade here at Minnisink Hills Regional Junior High School.

Now that I'd finally learned my way around this huge school, I was getting used to it. At first its size had terrified me, but then I realized its size was in my favor. Only the kids who were members of St. Martin's knew my father was a minister, and with four different towns sending to the school, not that many kids even went to St. Martin's. In Walkerton, everyone knew who I was and they had all called me Ruthie. Here, I'd made sure I was known as Ruth. Yes, things were looking up, especially now that Kenny Halberstrom had surfaced.

I was still thinking about Kenny when I opened the office door. As I handed my pass to one of the secretaries behind the counter, I noticed Mr. Burack, the principal, standing to one side with two men.

"Ruth Saunders is here, Mr. Burack," the secretary called over. Right away the other two secretaries stopped what they were doing and looked at me with funny expressions.

I was too surprised to register anything as Mr.

Burack and the two men walked over to me. One of the men opened his wallet and showed me a photograph of himself on some kind of official-looking ID card.

"I'm Lieutenant Janowitz. Are you the young lady who brought in sixty dollars cash this morning, all in tens?"

My mouth suddenly went cottony dry. I nodded, looking at Mr. Burack for reassurance. He smiled back, but somehow I didn't feel very reassured.

"I phoned your parents to explain what this was all about, Ruth, but I couldn't reach either of them. Suppose we go into my office where we can talk in private," he said.

The three secretaries were still staring as Mr. Burack ushered me into his office. Even with carpeting, the footsteps of the three men sounded as loud as drumbeats behind me.

·2·
THE NEARLY NEW

I SPENT THE REST OF THE DAY in shock. Counterfeit money—that was what those two men had wanted to see me about. One of my ten dollar bills had been counterfeit. I had to sign the bill for the bank records. It didn't look any different than any other bill, but I felt like some kind of master criminal putting my name to it. Not only that, but they kept the bill so I still owed ten dollars on my ski trips. I went to all my afternoon classes, but I doodled my way through them. I was a compulsive doodler. When something was bugging me, or even when it wasn't, I doodled swirls and curlicues and pictures all over everything.

I was just as glad Phyllis stayed after school for Band. Otherwise, I'd have had to talk to her all the way home on the bus, and I didn't feel like talking to anyone. Even so, the bus ride seemed to take forever. What a relief when St. Martin's loomed into sight. Loomed was a good word for it. St. Martin's was a huge, pinkish-red sandstone church, overgrown with dark ivy and surrounded by scrawny pine trees and limp-looking rhododendron. A straggly, thin hedge bordered the church property. Dad had painted all the doors red and planned to cut out some of the underbrush to make the place seem more cheerful, but I didn't see much hope for St. Martin's, with its turrets and towers and dark, old stained-glass windows, ever looking anything but gloomy. The date, 1889, was carved in the cornerstone. It must have been a big year for building dreary churches.

As our bus turned the corner by St. Martin's, I saw Dad standing on the church porch talking to Mr. Edmonds and some woman in a yellow raincoat. Though it was raining hard, Dad still wore only his work shirt and sweat pants. With the rain slivering down the bus windows, I knew he couldn't see me inside, but he smiled and waved as we drove past. Dad waved at all the school buses. He said by the law of averages he probably knew at least a couple of kids on any bus that went by. It usually embarrassed me, but today I didn't care.

Our front door was locked which was a big letdown. It meant Mom wasn't home, and I'd waited all day to tell her about the counterfeit bill. Besides, I didn't like going in the house alone. It was big and rambling, and on a rainy day like this, spooky. At least I had Tippy. As soon as I got the key from under the porch windowsill and let myself in, he barked a greeting. He used to leap with joy when I got home from school, but now that he was fourteen, he just lifted his head from where he lay on the floor and barked.

I dropped my books on the radiator and threw

myself down beside him. I rubbed his ears and snuggled my cheek against his soft neck. He kissed and licked my face in return. Mom didn't like him to do that, but Tippy was my friend, my very best friend. I used to tell people he was a Rhodesian Ridgeback because it sounded important, but now I knew he was important just being himself, a mutt. He had short hair with a white face, floppy ears, and an extra-long tail.

I turned over and rested my head on Tippy's shoulder. As I studied the cracks in the hall ceiling, I counted off where I'd gotten my six ten-dollar bills, just like I had this morning in Mr. Burack's office. Dad had given me a ten at breakfast as change for my two fives, that was one. Mrs. Cole, the church secretary, had paid me ten for baby-sitting, number two. The third I had gotten as change when I bought my skis at the St. Martin's Nearly New Shop. Aunt Nora had sent me a check for ten dollars for my birthday, which Dad had cashed for me, that was four. Mr. Edmonds had paid me ten dollars for two weeks of weeding at the church, and I'd been paid the sixth bill by the church office for helping at St. Martin's Nursery School. There it was, and all but the two tens Dad had given me had come from St. Martin's. And since Dad was the rector, I'd have to say all six came from St. Martin's.

"What do you think, Tip?" I asked.

Tippy's stomach growled in reply. Or maybe that was my stomach. I still hadn't had lunch and I suddenly realized I was famished. I rolled off Tippy and headed for the kitchen. Tippy struggled to his feet and followed me, panting from the effort. The kitchen was so dark, I had to turn on all the lights. Though the house belonged to St. Martin's and not to us, Mom had painted the woodwork and hung plants everywhere to make it look brighter. It didn't help much. Huge oak trees growing all around the house kept it forever dark.

Mom had left a note under my lunch bag on the counter. As I unwrapped my sandwich, I read it.

DEAR RUTH,

You must be hungry by now.

Janice called with wedding plans for us to go over. I'll be in New Haven until four tomorrow. Could you please take my place on clean-up at Nearly New this afternoon? Thanks.

Please bake the casserole in the fridge at 350 degrees for half an hour.

Love & a kiss,

MOM

Now I couldn't tell Mom about the counterfeit money until tomorrow.

I hadn't planned on eating dessert, but after reading Mom's note, I changed my mind. I was supposed to watch my weight. I watched it all right, mostly watched it go up. I wasn't fat, but I was certainly closer to fat than to thin. Mom told me to be patient, that when I got my growth spurt, I'd slim down. I was still waiting.

As soon as I finished off a bowl of chocolate pudding with whipped cream, I pulled on my slicker and ran down Wyndham Road two blocks to the church. St. Martin's property took up all four corners of where Wyndham Road crossed Hamilton Drive. The church itself was on one corner. Catty-corner was the Parish House, with parking lots on the other two corners. As I hurried past the church, I saw Dad still talking to Mr. Edmonds and the woman in the raincoat on the porch. I was dying to tell Dad what had happened in school, but not in front of anyone.

"Hey, Ruthie." Dad waved me over.

Ruthie! I had begged Dad not to call me Ruthie in public.

"Hi, there, Ruth." Mr. Edmonds waved, too. He was dressed in work clothes like Dad. He must have been helping Dad saw up the tree. Mr. Edmonds lived in a big house with a pool on a kind of estate. Dad said he had sold his business last summer and was moving to Arizona as soon as he sold his house. He didn't look old enough to retire to me. In fact, he looked Dad's age which I knew was fifty-four, only Mr. Edmonds was tall and really skinny, instead of short and sort of paunchy like Dad. Gardening and keeping the church grounds looking good was Mr. Edmonds's hobby, and he spent a lot of time at St. Martin's. Dad said that when Mr. Edmonds moved, the church would have to hire someone to do all the work that Mr. Edmonds did now for free.

Dad put his arm around my shoulders. "I'd like you to meet Florence Atkins, Ruthie, a clergyman . . ." Dad laughed. "My mistake, Florence, a clergyperson, right?"

As soon as Dad said that, I realized the woman wore a collar under her raincoat like Dad's. I was surprised. I'd never met an Episcopal woman minister before. Actually, she was pretty in a tall, big sort of way. She was, in fact, taller than Dad.

"Nice to meet you, Ruthie," she said as we shook hands.

"It's nice to meet you, too," I answered. "I have to run, Dad. Mom asked me to clean up for her at Nearly New, and I'm late already."

"Do you know your mother will be gone until tomorrow?"

I waved back a "yes" and splashed across Hamilton Drive and up the driveway to the Parish House. The Parish House was just an old house someone had donated to the church years ago. I couldn't imagine it ever being anyone's home. It was bumpy tan stucco with a Spanish-red tile roof and tall, narrow windows set deep into thick walls. It was so big, the nursery school took up the first floor, the Nearly New Shop the second, and Miss Kunzinger, the organist, lived on the third floor. I headed for the Nearly New side entrance.

The Nearly New Shop was only open on Wednesdays. People brought in their clothes and household goods for Nearly New to sell. They got most of the profit, with Nearly New keeping the rest for St. Martin's. Some of the customers were really characters, especially the regulars who showed up every week. I never minded working there, not when I could find great bargains like the skis I'd bought last month.

"Hello, Mrs. Moorehead," I said to the lady sitting at the cash register in a little alcove. "Mom had to go to New Haven so I'm taking her place."

"Good afternoon, Ruth." Mrs. Moorehead was totaling up price tags for a customer. "My, there must be lots of excitement in the Saunderses' house these days. I trust the wedding plans are going smoothly?"

Yuck, why didn't she just come out and ask why Mom had gone to New Haven? Mrs. Moorehead was syrupy sweet and smiled a lot, but never like she meant it. She must have been over fifty, like Mom, but her face had lots more lines, and her black hair was so oversprayed it looked plasticized.

I passed right over her question. "Do you want me in Coats?"

"Yes, please. I had hoped your father could move the coatracks for us, but he was busy with some woman minister . . ." Mrs. Moorehead shook her head in disapproval. ". . . woman minister. The whole idea is outrageous. Anyway, please straighten up in there, will you?"

I took off my slicker to hang it in the workers' closet. If anything was left around, anything at all, someone was sure to buy it. Mrs. Moorehead handed me her church key ring to unlock the door. Her key ring was just like Dad's, only the black label read "Women's Guild" instead of "Rector." I unlocked the closet and hung up my dripping slicker. As I slipped into a green, Nearly-New smock, Mrs. Moorehead signaled to me. Her customer had left.

"Ruth, I didn't want to discuss this in front of a stranger, but I think you should know that a Secret Service agent was in today questioning us about a counterfeit bill that *you* said you'd gotten here."

My heart picked up a beat. "Secret Service?"

"They said they were from the Treasury Department and were here to investigate counterfeit bills. They practically accused us of passing bad money. What in the world did you tell them?"

Now my heart was thudding against my ribs. Secret Service! "I . . . I handed in some money to the school today and one of my tens was counterfeit. I had to tell them where I'd gotten all my bills and . . . and I said one of them came from here."

"It's ridiculous. As if we'd have anything to do with counterfeit money."

I felt as if I were suffocating. "I'll go help in Coats." My voice was a croak.

Coats were at the end of the hall. Rows of pipe racks were crammed with coats of every size and color. Coats sold well in the fall, so the room was a mess where people had tried them on and then put them back any old way. I leaned my head against one of the racks to catch my breath.

"You, do you work here?" A short, fat woman holding a gray coat tapped my arm. She looked angry.

I managed to nod, but it was hard to focus on her.

"Look at this coat." The woman opened the coat, and I saw the lining was ripped all the way down the back. Otherwise, the coat looked new. "I won't pay more than five dollars for a coat in this condition," the woman snapped.

Oh, no! This was going to be trouble. Every once in a while a customer damaged goods just to get the price down, and I was in no mood for a hassle. I'd had hassle enough today.

I took the coat. "I'll show it to Mrs. Moorehead. She's in charge."

I cut through the Children's Room and headed for Household where Mrs. Moorehead sat in her alcove. As I turned the corner, I could see the cash register and a three-quarter view of Mrs. Moorehead's back, but she couldn't see me. The cash register drawer was open, and Mrs. Moorehead was taking bills out of it. She leaned down and picked up her pocketbook from under her stool. She opened it, jammed in the bills from the cash register, then took some bills out of her wallet and slipped them in the cash register drawer. She slammed the drawer shut and slid her pocketbook back under her stool, as if she were in a hurry.

She must have been hurrying because a customer was coming down the hall toward her, a tall, gray-haired woman carrying a pile of men's suits. It was Mrs. Gawler, a regular customer. I recognized her by her mustache. I'd always wondered if she shaved it.

The gray wool coat felt heavy as lead on my arm as I numbly watched Mrs. Moorehead total up Mrs. Gawler's suits. For sure, one of my ten dollar bills had come from this very cash register; and for sure, it could have been the counterfeit one. Maybe Mrs. Moorehead was taking real tens from the cash register and substituting counterfeit ones from her pocketbook.

I didn't like Mrs. Moorehead much. She was always phoning Dad to complain about something or other at the church. Still, she had been a member of St. Martin's forever. She sang in the choir, served on the Altar Guild, and this year ran the Nearly New Shop.

"Do you want something, Ruth?"

I jumped. Mrs. Moorehead was finished with the customer and had noticed me standing behind her. She seemed annoyed.

"It's . . . it's this coat," I stammered, holding out the damaged coat. "A customer says she won't pay full price for it."

While Mrs. Moorehead examined the coat, I mulled over what I'd just seen, suddenly catching myself up short. I was letting my imagination run away with me. Lots of the workers made change from the cash register. I'd even seen Mom do it a couple of times.

·3·
BABY-SITTER

WITH MOM IN NEW HAVEN, Dad and I ate in the kitchen instead of the dining room, which I liked because it made setting the table and cleaning up easy. And with Mom gone, I was able to tell Dad right away what had happened in school instead of listening to wedding talk for the whole meal. But Dad surprised me. He acted funny about my counterfeit bill, as if he didn't want to hear about it. He said the Secret Service had been to see him, and he already knew about it.

"But what about me getting all my ten dollar bills from St. Martin's, Dad?"

Dad passed it off. "I've heard lots of the stores uptown have been stuck with bad bills, Ruthie. It's a town-wide problem that is hurting everyone. Your counterfeit bill could have come from anywhere."

And that ended that. Maybe Dad wasn't interested because he was so wound up about that woman minister I'd met, Florence Atkins. He wanted to hire Florence as his new assistant. The last assistant had left in August, and Dad had been interviewing people ever since. If I needed something to get my mind off my counterfeit bill, that news did it. A woman assistant! Even I knew that women ministers had practically split the Episcopal Church in two. Why, Mrs. Moorehead had a fit just meeting Florence Atkins.

Dad was off on another crusade. I didn't know why I thought Fordwick, New Jersey would be any different from Walkerton, California, just because we'd been here six months and things had been peaceful. Six months of peace must be all that Dad could stand. Back in Walkerton, Dad had started a policy of opening the church buildings to outside groups, and some of the groups were pretty weird. The church members were plenty outspoken about what Dad was doing—one way or the other. Before long, the whole church was in an uproar. Because I knew Dad was right, it really bothered me to have people criticize him.

"Oh Dad, do you have to hire a woman assistant?"

"Why shouldn't I? I like her, and she's got the best qualifications of anyone so far." He tossed a scrap of meat to Tippy. "Everyone who's met her has been really impressed."

"But, Dad, people won't like . . ."

Ding-a-ling. Ding-a-ling. The phone interrupted me.

"I wish your friends wouldn't call between six and seven." Dad reached behind him for the wall phone before I could get to it.

"We're still eating, Phyllis. Can you call back, please?"

I frantically signaled that I was finished, but Dad had already hung up. It wasn't fair. He got more calls during dinner than I did.

Almost as if the phone had ESP, it rang again. Dad frowned as he picked it up.

"Oh, yes, Mrs. Cole, what is it?"

Mrs. Cole was the church secretary. Dad arranged his coffee cup in front of him as if he were in for a long conversation. "You want to speak to Ruthie?"

He couldn't help grinning as he handed me the phone. "I knew it would be for you."

"Ruth, Mr. Cole and I have an Environmental Board meeting tonight. Can you baby-sit until nine forty-five?" Mrs. Cole asked without even saying hello first.

Not 9:30 or 10 o'clock. But 9:45. That was Mrs. Cole all right. I covered the phone with my hand.

"Mrs. Cole wants me to sit tonight, Dad, just till nine forty-five. I still owe ten dollars on my ski trips. Please can I do it? Puh-leeze?"

Mom would never let me sit on a school night, but Dad just nodded, and went back to his coffee.

I quickly stacked, rinsed, and loaded our plates in the dishwasher. Mr. Cole was picking me up in fifteen minutes. Oliver Cole, age eight, and Lisa, age seven, were hard to handle, but tonight when I needed the money so badly, I couldn't be fussy. The Coles always paid me for every ten dollars worth of sitting, which I then had to work off. It was like blackmail, because I always owed them baby-sitting time, but right now the arrangement suited me fine. I was up to nine dollars which meant tonight I'd finish off the old ten and start on a new one. I'd turn it in to the school office first thing in the morning.

Mr. Cole picked me up right on time and drove me back to his house where Mrs. Cole was waiting with her coat on. The Coles looked more like brother and sister than husband and wife. They were both short and squarish and wore glasses. They were dark, too, though Mr. Cole's hair was black, and Mrs. Cole's hair was brown, streaked with lots of gray.

Oliver and Lisa were in their pajamas playing Chinese checkers on the new glass coffee table. The Coles had just papered, painted, carpeted, reupholstered, and decorated their whole house. Dad said Mr. Cole had a new job with a drafting equipment firm and was doing really well. I think Dad was worried that Mrs. Cole might quit as his secretary now that she didn't need the money, though why he wanted anyone around as super-organized as Mrs. Cole, I couldn't imagine.

She always gave me plenty of instructions. "We'll be at Town Hall, Ruth. The phone number, as well as the police, fire, doctor, and ambulance numbers are on the bulletin board as usual. I left your ten dollars on the desk. Be sure to call if anything comes up."

"Okay, Mrs. Cole. Thanks." I shut the door after them and turned to face Oliver and Lisa.

Oliver looked just like his mother, dark hair, dark eyes, glasses and all. "Your shoelaces aren't tied," he pointed out.

"They're not supposed to be." I dropped my books on the white and gold sofa. I never tied my shoelaces if I could get away with it.

"I'll play you a game as soon as I finish off Lisa," Oliver said, as he jumped three of Lisa's marbles and scooped them off the board. Lisa was dark, too, though she looked more like her father than her mother.

"No, thanks. I have to study for a math test." I picked up my math book. Only it wasn't my math book. I'd brought my health book by mistake. Still, even reading ahead in Health was better than playing Chinese checkers with Oliver. I'd played him once, and he'd beaten me so badly I'd felt like an idiot.

"Don't you two have homework?" I asked.

Both Oliver and Lisa had started private school this fall, and they were usually loaded with homework.

"We're going to the Guggenheim Museum tomorrow," Oliver said.

"Well, I have homework." Lisa jumped up and deliberately turned over the Chinese checker board. Marbles bounced and scattered all over the floor.

"You little creep." Oliver reached over and pounded Lisa on the arm.

Lisa let out with a terrible howl just as the phone rang.

"Answer that, will you please, Lisa?"

Oliver fell for the bait. As soon as Lisa headed for the phone, he raced around the desk and grabbed it first. The fight was over.

"No, my father isn't here," Oliver answered. "Yes, I'll take a message." He picked up a pencil and started to write as a voice on the other end dictated a message I couldn't hear.

Oliver was so efficient, I wondered why he needed a sitter. Maybe it was to keep him from killing his sister.

Bedtime took forever. I was supposed to read to Oliver and Lisa for half an hour before bed. Oliver had gotten a look at my health book and wanted to hear the chapter on reproduction, but I neatly avoided it. Mrs. Cole always assigned the reading, and right now we were struggling through a biography of Benjamin Franklin, and all hating it.

After I'd finally gotten both of them down, I checked

the refrigerator. In my hurry to finish the dishes, I'd skipped dessert, and now I was hungry. But the refrigerator was stocked with health food and fruit juices without a decent soft drink or sweet in sight. In desperation I ate a pear. Still hungry, I wandered back into the living room to watch an old Jerry Lewis movie on TV. I was just fiddling with the set to clear the picture when the phone rang. I rushed to answer it. All I needed was for Oliver and Lisa to wake up.

It was Phyllis. "Phyllis, how did you know I was here?" I whispered.

Without even thinking, I picked up a pencil from the desk and began to doodle on the bottom of Oliver's phone message for his father. I couldn't help noticing that Oliver's printing was neater than mine.

"When I called your house, your father said you were baby-sitting so I figured you were at the Coles'. Wait till you hear what I did."

"What?"

"I got my ears pierced."

"Phyllis, you didn't!" I shrieked, forgetting all about Oliver and Lisa. "Does your mother know?"

"Of course, she drove me to the mall. When she heard Dodie Beech got hers done, she decided it was socially acceptable. We just got back. I called you earlier to come with us, but your father said you were eating."

I drew a big earring on the paper. Having pierced ears was what Phyllis and I wanted more than anything else. Now that Phyllis had hers done, Mom just had to let me get mine pierced, too. Here I was, twelve years old, in Junior High, and still looking like a kindergartner.

Phyllis was really excited. "A nurse did it so it hardly

hurt. I have to wear gold studs for six weeks, then . . ."

I heard her, and yet I didn't hear her as I stared at the notepaper on the desk in front of me. It was stiff and crisp, not like any paper I'd ever written on before. Right beside it on the blotter was the ten dollar bill Mrs. Cole had left for me. I crinkled the bill between my fingers, then crinkled the notepaper. They both had the same crisp feel. Right away I remembered that the Coles had given me one of my ten dollar ski-trip bills as baby-sitting pay. Dad might have passed off my counterfeit ten as coming from anywhere, but not me. After all, I'd been the one who had to sign my name to it, not Dad.

Phyllis was still talking. "Do you think your mother will let you get yours done now?"

"Maybe." I slid both the notepaper and the ten dollar bill under the bright light of the desk lamp. The notepaper and the bill looked alike, but the money had little colored lines running through it that the notepaper didn't have. They weren't the same after all.

·4·
SEARCH FOR POSTER PAPER

WHEN I GOT HOME FROM THE COLES' that night, Dad was at a meeting, and he was still asleep when I left for school in the morning so I had no chance to talk things over with him. At least I had the ten dollars ski-trip money, and I could tell Mom everything when she got home from New Haven that afternoon.

But when I got off the bus after school, not only did I find Mom home, but Janice and her two roommates as well. They'd arrived for the weekend to have their bridesmaids' dresses fitted. Janice looked fantastic. Her hair was brown and straight like mine, but she'd had it cut short so it curled up at the ends. And she wore new, big, tinted eyeglasses that were totally glamorous.

Right away I told Mom about my counterfeit bill and how I'd been called into the school office. She said she was sorry I was out the ten dollars, but she passed it off as no-big-deal, just like Dad had. She must have been too busy to realize what a trauma I'd been through.

It wasn't just Mom who was busy. We all were. What with getting our dresses fitted, deciding on our bouquets, addressing and stamping the invitations, and setting up a room for the wedding presents, we ran around like crazy. Because the wedding was the Saturday before Thanksgiving, we were wearing fall colors. The bridesmaids' dresses were Damson Plum, and the maid of honor's dress was Cinnamon. If I'd been taller, I just bet I'd have been maid of honor instead of a bridesmaid. Well, I was first down the aisle anyway, and the floor-length dresses were great—high in front and low in back with a filmy cape that hid my not-so-tiny waistline. Mom was going to let me wear a padded bra, and Tom's sister promised to make up my eyes the day of the wedding. I couldn't wait to show Phyllis our big floppy hats. They were spectacular.

I told Mom all I needed to look completely grown-up were pierced ears. She wasn't too busy to register on that. What Phyllis did was the Leggetts' decision, but Mom's decision was that I wasn't "mature" enough for pierced ears. Maybe when I showed a sense of responsibility toward schoolwork, keeping my clothes and room neat, and remembering my chores without being reminded, she and Dad would consider it. Maybe.

Late Sunday night, Janice and her friends went back to New Haven and reality set in. Monday was dismal, with more rain. When I left California, my friends had said it rained all the time in New Jersey, and I was beginning to think they were right. And I was getting another cold, my second this fall. To make the day even drearier, when I got home from school, the house was empty. Tippy was so exhausted from the frantic weekend, he didn't even wake up when I unlocked the front door.

I turned on the lights. I'd never get used to such a dark house. Dad had said it was eighty years old. Maybe people in those days liked dark houses, but I sure didn't. In Walkerton, we'd lived in a ranch house with big picture windows that was light all day long, and I missed it.

I sneezed twice and blew my nose. My whole head was clogged up. Maybe some orange juice would help. I wandered into the kitchen, drank two glasses of juice, and then looked around for the poster paper Dad had said he'd bring home from the church. I needed it for my art collage that was due tomorrow.

The poster paper wasn't in the kitchen. All I found was a note from Mom that she'd gone to work. Mom worked part-time at the Yarn Barn, a needlepoint shop in town, with the hopes they'd hire her full time. I knew money was tight for Mom and Dad. Janice's education had been really expensive, and last year Dad's father who was ninety-one went into a nursing home that Dad said cost an incredible amount.

I finished the apple pie left over from the weekend, washed it down with more orange juice, then searched the house for the poster paper. It wasn't in the den, the living room, my bedroom, or anywhere else. Dad must have forgotten it. I wasn't surprised. Dad and I were alike that way, only he didn't get in trouble—which was what would happen to me if I didn't get that collage done. I'd have to go down to the church and pick up the poster paper myself.

I pulled on my still-wet slicker and ran down the hill.

The trees were dripping, and the road underfoot was slick with wet leaves. I saw Dad's blue Toyota in the church parking lot. Good, that meant he was in his office. But the Toyota's front window was wide open, and it was pouring. I splashed through the parking lot, soaking my sneakers right through to my socks, and rolled up the car window, wishing Mom could see how responsible I was. It was lucky Dad hadn't left his back window open too. The back seat was stacked with cardboard cartons that were sealed and resealed, as if the crown jewels were packed inside.

I cut across the soggy lawn and entered the side door of the church. I turned on the hall light, pulled open the heavy oak door that led into the church itself, and peeked in. St. Martin's was dark like our house on a rainy day, only it was even gloomier. And it always smelled of candlewax, stale flowers, and the musty old red velvet pew cushions. It was an echoey kind of stone church, damp and cold, with a three-story-high ceiling, supported by enormous stone pillars that even Samson would have found hard to knock down. Tarnished brass In Memoriam plaques covered the dark wood beams and shiny scratched pews. Dad thought a good steam cleaning would brighten the stonework, but so little light filtered through the big stained-glass windows, I didn't see how even a thousand gallons of white paint would help.

I'd heard people call St. Martin's a beautiful church. Maybe when I got used to its dreary 1889-ness, I'd think so too. Certainly Dad had been pleased to come here, and so had Mom. St. Martin's was much bigger than Trinity Church in Walkerton, and I knew Dad's salary was bigger as well. Besides, both Mom and Dad had been born in Connecticut and were glad to be back East.

I let the heavy oak door swing shut, and, with the slip-slap of rain on the slate roof above me, I headed down the worn blue carpeting toward the offices. The church itself took up about half of the huge stone building. The other half included the big Seabury Reception Room, with a kitchen and pantry off it, the Altar Guild Room, the Choir Room, and the offices, all surrounding a center courtyard like a doughnut circles a hole.

Actually, it wasn't a courtyard, it was a columbarium. I didn't even know what a columbarium was until I came to St. Martin's. It was a cemetery for people's ashes. After a body was cremated, the ashes were buried in urns in the ground. The columbarium was Mr. Edmonds's special project, and he never let anyone else take care of it. Though it always looked neat, with clipped shrubs and border gardens and flagstone walks with stone benches for sitting, it gave me the shivers even more than a regular cemetery, especially on a dismal day like this. Maybe that was because a cemetery didn't pretend to be anything but a cemetery, while a columbarium tried to pass itself off as some kind of mini-park.

The building was quiet on Mondays. There were no women sewing or cooking, no AA meetings or retired men's luncheons, no Bible study groups or choir rehearsals that usually kept the church buzzing. So I was surprised to hear men's voices as I passed the Seabury Room. When I stuck my head in the doorway, I saw a bar of light shining from the open basement door.

"What are you doing down here, Lou? I've been waiting for you to help me cut up that tree by the parking lot."

There was no mistaking Mr. Edmonds's deep, bass voice coming up the basement stairs.

"I'm busy. I'll come when I can," Lou muttered.

"And when do you think that will be?" Mr. Edmonds's tone was mock-respectful.

I didn't wait to hear more. Their arguing didn't interest me. Dad had hired Lou Dargie last summer as the church sexton to clean and do odd jobs. I knew that Mr. Edmonds didn't like him, and I wasn't sure I liked him myself. Lou never spoke to me, not even to say hello. But then, he wasn't friendly with anyone. He was great at doing what Dad asked him to do, but when anyone else gave him orders, he didn't exactly knock himself out. Lou's coloring was so fair, he hardly had any eyebrows or eyelashes at all. I'd never been able to figure out if his hair was blond or white. Everything about him looked bland and pale, except for his blue eyes that practically blazed through a person.

I had never given a thought to where Lou lived until one day when I saw a green van pick him up by the railroad station. H. C. C. C. was painted in yellow on the van doors. I decided that must stand for Harrison County Country Club, only Lou didn't seem much like the country-club type to me. Maybe he lived over the club garages.

I was still thinking about Lou as I turned the corner toward the offices. Mrs. Cole's office was empty, and Dad's door was shut. I was never to go into Dad's office without knocking. Someone might be telling Dad about a terrible problem, or some kid might be in there trying to kick drugs, or maybe Dad was just taking a nap. Whatever, Dad's office was private with a capital "P." I gave the door a timid knock.

"Who's there?"

"It's me, Ruth."

"Come in."

Because I had expected Dad to be alone, I was surprised to see Mrs. Cole standing in front of Dad's desk, dressed in her coat and holding an armful of books. Both Dad and Mrs. Cole's expressions were blank with shock, as if they had just seen an accident.

"Well, what is it, Ruthie?" Dad demanded.

As they stared at me, I felt a sneeze coming on. "I need the poster paper, Dad. You said you'd bring it home."

Kercheeew! I let out with a beauty. Now my nose was running, and I had no Kleenex.

Dad looked puzzled, but Mrs. Cole seemed to know what I was talking about. "Something's come up, Ruth. I'll get it for you in a few minutes."

"No." Dad barked. His face was red all the way up to, and including, his bald head. It was as if his round collar were choking him.

"But Dad, I need it for . . ."

"We're busy. Run along." Dad reached for the candy jar on his desk, and unwrapped a sour ball. When Dad gave up smoking last year, he started eating candy instead. Now he was trying to give up candy.

"I'll make sure your father brings home the poster paper tonight." Mrs. Cole began to shoo me out the door with little fluttering motions, as if I were some kind of pest she was trying to get rid of. As she edged me toward the door, I noticed Hammond Trust Company was stamped on the books she held under her arm. Bank books. I wondered if Dad and Mrs. Cole were upset about something in the bank books. It was possible. I'd heard in school today that more counterfeit bills had turned up in Fordwick over the weekend.

I stopped at the door and looked back at Dad. He was putting on his coat. "Dad, did you hear about more coun . . ."

"Ruth, will you please go home. I have to go to the bank before it closes."

Poster paper or no poster paper, I'd better get going. Dad almost never spoke to me that way, but when he did, I knew he meant it. I backed up fast and pulled his office door shut behind me. Something terrible must have happened.

·5·
THE EAVESDROPPER

DINNER WAS QUIET. Mom said she was tired from the weekend and working all day, and Dad was grimly silent. For once, he didn't eat his dessert. I felt so rotten with my cold, I didn't eat mine either. Plus, I was worried about Dad.

"Dad's really upset about something, Mom. What is it?" I asked, as soon as we were alone in the kitchen.

"I have no idea. He said a problem had come up at the church that he'll tell me about later."

I put on rubber gloves to wash the pots and pans. I'd read an article in *Seventeen* about how dishwashing detergents can prematurely age the hands. "When I was in Dad's office today, Mrs. Cole was there with a lot of bank books, and she was upset, too."

Mom came over to the sink and put her arms around me. "Dad's perfectly capable of taking care of the church without our help, Ruthie. Now stop worrying, hear?" She scooped up my long hair, piled it on top of my head, and kissed me in the hollow of the neck the way she used to when I was little.

I shook my head. "I'm too old for that."

"You'll never be too old for that."

No one around here took me seriously. Still, with Mom in a mellow mood, this might be a good time to discuss a few things. "What do you think about me getting my hair cut, Mom?"

"You mean like Janice's?"

"Maybe even shorter. With those big bridesmaids' hats, short hair would be great, and I know it would make my face look thinner." I finished the last pan and pulled off my gloves.

Mom held up my hair as if she were considering it. "I think it would be sensational. If your cold's better, I'll take you to get it cut tomorrow."

Mom was really mellow. "I just have a stuffy nose, Mom, that's all. And pierced ears would look good with short hair, don't you think?"

"Short hair, yes, pierced ears, no. I've told you that pierced ears are a privilege to be earned. Period."

I should have guessed that Mom wasn't that mellow. Well, if she wanted responsible, I'd show her responsible. After I scoured the sink and started the dishwasher, I tucked in my shirttails and tied my shoelaces. Then I hurried into the front hall and gathered up my books, gym bag, and the poster paper that Dad had finally brought home. As I passed the den on my way back to the kitchen, I noticed Dad slumped in his favorite chair, the open newspaper in his lap, listening to WQXR on his radio. He looked depressed. Lots of nights after dinner Dad and I played backgammon. He almost always beat me, but I was learning. Lately we hadn't played backgammon at all. Something serious was bugging Dad, no matter what Mom said.

When I got back to the kitchen, Mom was putting on her coat. "I promised to help set up for the church luncheon tomorrow. I'll be home by nine."

I dumped everything on the kitchen table. "I'm all organized, Mom. First I'm going to wash my gym stuff, then I'll start on art."

At least that made an impression. Mom smiled her approval as she headed for the den to say good-bye to Dad. I saw no point in mentioning that I'd already been dropped a whole grade in touch football because my gym things hadn't passed inspection.

As soon as Mom left, I blew my nose hard and sneezed the sneeze I'd been holding in. My throat hurt, too. What I felt like was going to bed. Instead, I picked up my gym bag and headed for the washing machine in the basement.

Our basement was hopeless. It had a plain concrete floor with pipes and wires and extension cords hanging all over the place. Dad's tools, the washer and dryer, an old, wheezing freezer the last minister had left behind, shelves of food Mom had canned, and just plain junk filled the whole space. When we first moved in, I wanted to fix up a playroom like the Coles', but every time it rained hard, the basement leaked. That ended those plans.

I pulled out the knob to start the washing machine, but only a trickle of water dribbled in. I'd forgotten the dishwasher was on. Our plumbing was so ancient, if one appliance was running, there wasn't enough pressure for any other. And I was cold. Dad hadn't turned on the furnace yet, and with all our rain, the basement was damp and chilly. Shivering, I blew my nose again and waited for the tub to fill. From above my head, I heard the loud sound of Dad's radio. I looked up. An old, no-longer used hot-air register was right over the washing machine. It must have led straight up into the den.

At last the tub was full. Just as I threw in my dirty gym suit, sweatshirt, socks, sneakers, and towels, I heard the front doorbell ring. Tippy started barking like crazy.

"Well, Chief, it's good to see you. How've you been?"

It was Dad's voice right above me, coming down the register as clear as if he were broadcasting. "Chief" must be Police Chief Nussen. What was the police chief doing here? I couldn't ever remember a policeman coming to our house before. I swallowed carefully past the raw soreness of my throat. Upstairs I heard the radio volume being lowered. Automatically, I pushed in the knob to stop the swish-swish of the wash cycle. The basement was instantly silent, except for our resident cricket. It had been chirping away somewhere in our basement for three days now. I wondered if Dad could hear the cricket as clearly as I could hear him.

"I guess you know why I've come, Mr. Saunders," the chief said. It was weird to hear a strange voice without seeing it connected to a body. "Since the whole situation is out of my jurisdiction, I'm here strictly as a friend, and, of course, as a member of St. Martin's."

"I appreciate that, Chief. Sit down."

I shouldn't have listened. I knew I shouldn't have. It was like reading someone else's mail, or going through their bureau drawers. I should have marched upstairs and started my homework. But I just had to know what was going on. Not daring to blow my nose for fear they would hear me, I stifled a sneeze and wiped the drip off the end of my nose with a Kleenex.

"Frankly, I'm concerned about St. Martin's, Mr. Saunders. I'm sure you know that people are talking, and this sort of thing hurts the church. Fordwick is a conservative suburban town, and we're set in our ways. Right or wrong, appearances are important to us. I'll be honest, Mr. Saunders, you're new, with a reputation for being pretty liberal, and until people get to know you, they're apt to be cautious."

"I'm as concerned about this as you are, Chief, only more so. I'll welcome any help you can give me."

I rubbed my goose-pimply arms to warm them. Something was wrong. I could tell by the super-polite way the police chief was talking.

"By regulation, the Treasury Department is in charge, though they plan to keep our department posted," he went on. "I just want to warn you that when the Secret Service interviews you tomorrow, they'll be looking into you and your background pretty closely. As a friend and a parishioner, I urge you to cooperate. There's not enough evidence for a search warrant, but it might be to your benefit to let them search the church property."

"There's no need for that. I've already searched the grounds and buildings thoroughly myself." Dad's voice was curt. "Besides, Chief, you know as well as I do that counterfeit bills have turned up elsewhere in Fordwick, not just at St. Martin's."

Counterfeit money! St. Martin's *was* somehow involved with counterfeit money. And Chief Nussen's nicey-nice tone almost made it sound as if he suspected Dad. Not only that, but he'd said people were talking about Dad and the church, just like they had back in Walkerton. It wasn't fair. Dad hadn't done a thing for people to talk about. For a long moment all I could hear was our basement cricket and the turned-down music of Dad's radio above me. Then a chair was pushed back on the still-uncarpeted den floor.

"I know it wasn't easy for you to come here, Chief, and I appreciate it. Thank you," I heard Dad say, super-polite himself.

Another chair scraped across the floor, and I figured they were both standing up.

"Incidentally, the Secret Service is aware of the Lou Dargie setup, and they'll be checking that out . . ." As the chief's voice trailed off, I pulled out the washing-machine knob and watched my gym things churn into a sudsy boil. Lou Dargie. What did Lou Dargie have to do with this? Dad had to tell me what was going on, that's all there was to it. I ran up the basement stairs and into the front hall just as Dad closed the door behind Chief Nussen.

"Dad, what's happening? I have to know." My eyes brimmed over, and I didn't know whether that was from tears or from my cold.

Dad studied me, watery eyes, red nose, frown and all. Then he led me back into the den, sat me down, and pulled his chair close to mine. Tippy hobbled across the room and lay down on the floor between us.

Dad put his hand on my knee. "You're right, Ruthie, you should know. After all, you were stuck with a bad bill yourself. When you were in my office today, Mrs. Cole had just come back from the bank. The teller discovered over two hundred dollars' worth of counterfeit tens in our Sunday offering."

Two hundred dollars! That was a lot of money. No wonder Dad was uptight.

"Maybe Lou Dargie had something to do with it, Dad." It was just a guess.

Dad put his hand under my chin and tilted my face up so I was looking straight into his eyes. "You were eavesdropping on the chief and me that whole time, weren't you? I can't tell you how disappointing that is to me, Ruthie. You have no idea what this is all about. What you heard was only a small part of the whole story, and innocent people get hurt that way. This business doesn't concern you, and I want to make it very clear that you are not to meddle in any way. Do you understand?"

I nodded, then let out with a huge sneeze that sprayed all over everything. Dad passed me his handkerchief and I blew. I had been wrong to eavesdrop, and I was sorry, especially when I saw what deep worry lines wrinkled Dad's forehead. When I pictured Dad, I always pictured him laughing, but I hadn't heard him laugh in a long time.

As I handed back his handkerchief, for some reason I thought of those sealed cartons I'd seen in the back of his car today. To someone who didn't know Dad, they might have looked suspicious, and I'd just bet the Secret Service already suspected Dad. That must have been what Chief Nussen was hinting at. After all, they knew that Dad had given me two of my ten dollar bills as change, and they probably knew how much Dad needed money right now, too. Not only that, but I bet they thought that Dad was the only one who handled the offering money. I hoped Dad set them straight. Lots of people could get their hands on that offering: the ushers, the Altar Guild, the money counters, the choir, the organist, the acolytes.

All of a sudden, I had a really bad, skull-pounding headache. And I was terribly hot. I didn't know whether that was because I was sick or burning mad. It was probably both. I certainly felt rotten, but I was steamed up, too. Why should Dad have to defend himself to Chief Nussen, the Secret Service, or anyone else, when he'd never, ever, done a dishonest thing in his whole life?

·6·
KENNY'S PURCHASE

WHEN I WOKE UP THE NEXT MORNING, I felt even worse than I had the night before. I didn't have a cold. I had flu. For the rest of the week I was so knocked out, I didn't watch TV or read or do anything. I didn't even remember about the Secret Service until Friday, but when I asked Dad about it, he gave his usual half-answer, which didn't tell me anything at all. He just wasn't going to discuss it. At that point, I was too sick to press. Then by Sunday, I was having a hard enough time convincing Mom and Dad to let me go to school the next day, without pestering them about anything else.

On Monday I didn't feel all that great. In fact, by lunchtime I was pretty shaky. I was in the cafeteria line loading up my tray in the hopes that food would revive me when I heard a deep voice, practically in my ear. "Are untied shoelaces your trademark or something?"

There weren't that many deep voices in Minnisink

Hills Regional Junior High School. I turned around. It was Kenny Halberstrom behind me in line. THE Kenny Halberstrom.

"Yeah, that's how my friends recognize me." I surprised myself by my fast comeback, and I surprised myself even more by not blushing.

"You're Ruth Saunders, aren't you? Are you going on the ski trips?"

"Yeah, I can't wait. Are you?"

"Yeah, but I don't have any skis. I guess I'll have to rent."

I couldn't believe I was talking to Kenny Halberstrom. Kenny Halberstrom! Maybe I was still sick and hallucinating. I took a long time picking out dessert, just as if I didn't love angel cake. I could afford to treat myself. I'd not only lost four days of school with the flu, I'd also lost four pounds.

"I bought really cheap Head skis at St. Martin's Nearly New Shop. Do you go to St. Martin's?" I'd never seen him there, but that didn't mean anything.

Kenny reached for a piece of pumpkin pie, and I automatically took one too, though I hate pumpkin. "No, I go to Central Presbyterian," he said.

Good, maybe he didn't know that Dad was a minister. "Nearly New has got more skis for sale at a good price. They'll even hold them for you on deposit . . ." I trailed my sentence off as I headed for a table with two empty seats.

It worked. Kenny followed right after me and put his tray down so fast, his chili slopped over. "Where is this place?"

"It's a thrift shop run by St. Martin's right down the street from where I live. It's open on Wednesdays." I took my sandwich out of my bag and started to eat.

"I've only lived in Clarkston a year. Where's St. Martin's?"

Even better. Clarkston was two towns away from Fordwick. "It's about half a mile up from the Fordwick railroad station. Take a right on Tobert . . . no, I mean a left. . . ."

Kenny interrupted me. "If you live near the place, why don't I come home Wednesday on your bus, and you can show me?"

Come home with me! I swallowed a bite of sandwich the wrong way and nearly gagged. By the time I'd finished coughing, my eyes were red and so was my face. "That's okay with me," I managed to get out.

When the bell rang, I went to English instead of art. I wasn't sure whether it was the flu or Kenny that had me in such a daze. Whichever, I couldn't wait to tell Phyllis in seventh-period study.

"Phyllis, I had lunch with Kenny Halberstrom. He's coming home on our bus Wednesday to buy skis at the Nearly New. He's adorable. He has hazel eyes. His voice has changed. I think he shaves."

Phyllis's mouth practically dropped open. "Kenny Halberstrom! Maybe I'll skip Band and come home on the bus with you."

In one way I wanted Phyllis to come. She always knew what to talk about. In another way, I didn't. Ever since she'd had her ears pierced, she had been putting on mascara and blush on the way to school. She looked at least like an eighth grader, and with me stuck home sick all week, I hadn't even gotten my hair cut yet.

When Wednesday came, Phyllis finally decided to stay for Band. I was just as glad, and it wasn't that hard to talk to Kenny after all. He was crazy about soccer and had just made the eighth-grade team. I could even discuss it semi-intelligently. Phyllis's brother was on the high school varsity, and I'd been to a couple of games with Phyllis and her parents. We talked about soccer for the whole twenty-minute bus trip.

Then we were on Wyndham Road, standing in the drizzle. The bus door swooshed shut behind us. Me, alone with Kenny Halberstrom. I just hoped Dad didn't show up wearing his collar and calling me Ruthie, or worse, Baby.

"There's our house." I pointed down the street.

"Man, that's great." Kenny sounded like he meant it. I had never thought of our house as great before, just as big and old and dark with a gross green paint job, the same as the falling-down, old garage out back that used to be a barn.

The front door was unlocked. "Mom?"

When Tippy saw Kenny, he leapt into his usual barking act. Instead of backing off like most people, Kenny knelt right down and patted him as if he knew Tippy was an old fake.

Mom came out of the den wearing her glasses and carrying a newspaper. I had to give her credit. She didn't even blink when she saw Kenny in our front hall. I introduced them.

"Nice to meet you, Kenny." Mom smiled, and they shook hands. Then Mom handed me the newspaper. "The local paper got wind of Janice being home last weekend and wrote it up in their social column. You're mentioned, too, Ruth."

Grateful for the Ruth instead of Ruthie, I grabbed the paper as Mom explained to Kenny about the wedding next month. I quickly read the article. Oh, no. It said that Dad was rector of St. Martin's, and there was my name listed as junior bridesmaid. Where did they get that junior nonsense? I handed the paper back to Mom, hoping Kenny would never see it.

Kenny and I had some cookies and cider, then walked down the street to the Parish House. Though it had stopped raining, big gray clouds scudded across a gray sky.

We crossed Hamilton Drive a few steps behind Lou Dargie. He was on his way to the Nearly New with a big carton of books. I hadn't seen or thought of Lou in over a week, but now I remembered how Chief Nussen had mentioned the Lou Dargie setup, whatever that was. As we followed Lou up the stairs to Nearly New, a policeman at the top greeted him.

"Hey there, Lou, how's it going?"

Lou grunted without answering.

"What's a cop doing here?" Kenny whispered.

"There's been some shoplifting lately, so a cop walks through a couple of times a day to keep everyone on their toes."

As Kenny and I turned into Toys and Sports, I saw Mrs. Moorehead in her usual place behind the cash register. She was too busy checking out a woman buying Halloween costumes to notice us. Halloween outfits were big sellers in October.

"There're the skis," I said, which was stupid, because they were stacked against the wall in plain sight.

Kenny started to sort through them. He picked out a pair of K 2's and measured them against his forehead. "Man, these are terrific. Do you think five dollars will hold them on deposit for a couple of weeks?"

"Sure, they're . . ."

"Look out." Lou pushed past us carrying a big electric typewriter with a "Hold" sticker on it. Lou was thin, and shorter than Kenny, but he had to be strong to lift that heavy typewriter. He unlocked the closet in the back of the room that was used for deposit items and set the typewriter on a shelf.

"Could you please leave the closet open, Lou?" I asked. "These skis are going in there on deposit."

"No, I gotta leave now."

I made a face at Kenny to apologize for Lou's rudeness as Lou locked up the closet, then clipped his Sexton's key ring back on his belt.

Kenny had already put the K 2's to one side and started to sort through the pile of ski poles when I heard a woman's angry voice down the hall. At first it was low, but then it began to rise hysterically. I'd worked at Nearly New enough to know trouble when I heard it. A couple of Nearly-New ladies in their green smocks hurried by. Kenny didn't notice the commotion, but as soon as he picked up his skis and poles, and we went out into the hall, he couldn't miss it. A little cluster of people were gathered around the policeman down by Coats. Though they all seemed to be talking at once, a tall woman in the middle was talking the loudest. I recognized her right away by her mustache. It was Mrs. Gawler.

Kenny jerked his thumb toward the group. "What's with her?"

I tried to pass it off with a shrug. "I dunno."

More Nearly-New ladies gathered around like a flock of cackling geese. The cop held up his hands. "Please, ladies, please."

Gradually the racket quieted. All but Mrs. Gawler. She shook her finger at the policeman. "You gotta do something about this place. I was pulled in for passing bad ten dollar bills. And I'll tell you where I got 'em. Right here. Two weeks ago I got two tens in change from my fifty dollar bill. Those were the bad tens, I know it. What kind of church is this anyway, getting decent people like me in trouble?"

"What's she talking about?" Kenny asked.

"You wouldn't believe the weird people who come in here." I tried to laugh it off, but my throat was scratchy tight as I steered Kenny toward the cash register alcove. "Mrs. Moorehead, can we pay . . ." I stopped. It wasn't Mrs. Moorehead behind the cash register. It was a woman I recognized, but whose name I didn't remember.

"I'll help you, Ruth," the woman said. "Mrs. Moorehead thought there was so much cash in the register, she'd better get it up to the bank

Kenny handed over his five dollars. "Can I hold these skis and poles on deposit for a couple of weeks?"

The woman nodded, took Kenny's money, then frowned up at me. "Honestly, Ruth, I don't know what's happened to St. Martin's. First, Secret Service men are in here questioning everyone about counterfeit money, and now we have this upset today. I think your fa . . ."

Rude or not, I had to cut her off. There was absolutely no way I was going to listen to her opinion about Dad, especially in front of Kenny. "Can we have the keys for the deposit closet, please?"

As the woman handed me the keys, Kenny put away his wallet. "If I ever get change from here, remind me to have it X-rayed."

I laughed as if it were the best joke I'd ever heard, but I knew there was nothing funny about it.

·7·
A DRIVE IN
THE COUNTRY

B Y THE END OF THE WEEK, I decided I was at last over the flu, and when I got my hair cut on Thursday, I felt really better. It was short, collar length, and I loved the way it tickled my bare neck. Both Mom and I agreed that my face looked definitely thinner with short hair. If nothing else, my new haircut helped take my mind off what had happened at the Nearly New. When I asked Dad how the whole thing had ended, he said he'd come over from his office and agreed with Mrs. Gawler that she had a right to be angry about the counterfeit bills. However, unless she had proof they came from the Nearly New, she should drop the matter. Then he paid her twenty dollars out of his own money, with the hope she'd return as a valued customer. It seemed to satisfy her.

On Friday, I ate lunch with Kenny. He didn't mention my hair, which was annoying, but he didn't mention the uproar at the Nearly New either, which more than made up for it. Instead, we talked about his soccer team and the ninth-grade Talent Show we'd had in Assembly that morning. The lunch bell rang much too soon.

The next day, Saturday, I raced around all morning to finish my chores before the Leggetts picked me up to drive to the away–high-school soccer game at Dunbridge High School, wherever that was. While I was bolting down a quick lunch, Dad came in from raking leaves and joined Mom and me for a cup of coffee. Even though he had on his sweat pants and socks-over-his-boots outfit, his cheeks were red from working outside, and he didn't look as tired as he had lately. Yesterday afternoon, when I'd ridden my bike to the library, I'd noticed his blue Toyota parked outside the police station. It had given me a real jolt, but when I'd asked him about it later, he'd just shaken his head, and wouldn't discuss it. Last night we'd had one of those silent dinners, but this morning Dad seemed determined to be cheerful.

With Tippy asleep under the table, the three of us talked over our latest wedding crisis, whether Dad should take Janice down the aisle as father of the bride, or marry Janice and Tom as their minister. Dad said he could only be father of the bride twice in his life and that's what he wanted to do. Mom thought Dad should perform the ceremony. I thought he should do both, walk Janice down the aisle, then quick put on his robes and do the wedding, too.

"Thanks for the coffee, Grace. I've got to run." Dad put his mug in the sink before we reached a decision. "I'm seeing Gordon Bayley at twelve-thirty about those letters."

I knew that Gordon Bayley was Bishop Bayley.

"What letters, Mom?" I asked as soon as Dad had left.
She didn't answer.

"Mom, tell me."

"I can't imagine why your father even mentioned it. It's all a tempest in a teapot." Mom sounded annoyed as she finished her coffee. "A few members of St. Martin's have gotten together and written letters to Bishop Bayley. It's just a small group of old-timers who wanted someone more conservative than your father as rector expressing their disapproval. Plus, they're upset about the possibility of a woman assistant. You know as well as I do, Ruthie, that the less attention paid to this sort of thing, the faster it blows over."

Letters! That was a new one. Talk was one thing, but letters was another. It sounded so . . . so permanent, like everything was on record. I just bet Mrs. Moorehead was in on it. She was the biggest letter writer around. She was always writing letters to our town newspaper to complain about unleashed dogs, potholes in the streets, or uncollected garbage. Mom was probably right, it was just a few people stirring things up, but I knew from Walkerton that just a few troublemakers like Mrs. Moorehead could make a lot of trouble. Well, Bishop Bayley was a friend of Dad's. I'd just have to count on him being smart enough not to listen to dumb gossip.

I hardly had time to eat lunch. I was sure the Leggetts would be early, and they were. Dr. Leggett was always early. He wasn't a doctor-doctor, he was an educator-doctor at the local state college. As usual, as soon as I got in the Leggetts' car, Phyllis pumped me about my Band raffle tickets. Though I hadn't sold a one, I told Phyllis I was doing fine. As a matter of fact, the only time I remembered the tickets was when Phyllis asked me about them. They were still in my slicker pocket.

"Have I got something to tell you about Kenny Halberstrom," Phyllis announced when we'd finished the Band raffle business.

"What? Is he coming to the game today?"

"I don't know. But when I was in the library uptown this morning, Kenny and Paul Sutton were there, and I heard them talking about you." Phyllis paused and fiddled with her earrings as if they needed tightening or something.

I knew she wanted me to beg her. I usually didn't play that game, but for once, I couldn't resist. "What did they say?" I tried not to sound too eager.

"Kenny was wondering if you were going to Jake Belson's party next Saturday night."

"He didn't!" Jake was in the eighth grade, like Kenny, and he gave parties all the time.

"Yes, he did, and he sounded like he might be interested in you." Phyllis could afford to be generous. The day after Kenny came home on the bus with me, Phyllis had decided she liked Matt Davis better. Matt was just about the tallest boy in the whole Junior High.

"Did he say anything about what happened with the counterfeit money at the Nearly New?" Hopefully, Kenny had forgotten all about it.

"No, they were just talking about the party . . ."

"What about the counterfeit money, Ruth?" Dr. Leggett interrupted. "I understand that St. Martin's has had a lot of trouble. What does your father say about it?"

I had forgotten all about the Leggetts sitting up front. I flushed crimson. "I don't know, Dr. Leggett. Dad never talks about it." That was true enough.

"From what I hear, this counterfeiter is pretty smart. It's usually greed that trips up a counterfeiter, but apparently this one is making only what he needs."

Mrs. Leggett turned around in her seat. "One of our neighbors was handed two counterfeit tens yesterday at Minnisink Flowerland. She used to be a bank teller so she spotted them right away. She and the florist took them straight to the police."

St. Martin's bought their altar flowers at Minnisink Flowerland every Friday. Maybe that's why Dad was at the police station yesterday. But that was silly. Lots of people shopped there, not just St. Martin's.

Still, it was hard to shake the coincidence from my mind. I could have kicked myself for bringing up the subject, and knowing Dr. Leggett, I had a hunch he wasn't finished.

He wasn't. "My father had a print shop for thirty years so I know a good deal about the printing business. The biggest problem for counterfeiters has always been the paper. The paper used for making money is just a standard hundred percent rag paper that can be bought anywhere. But the Treasury Department paper has special colored silk fibers running through it that can't be duplicated. Only one manufacturer in the United States produces it, and when it's shipped to the mint, it travels under armed guard. Counterfeiters just have to make do with plain rag paper."

Dr. Leggett pulled out a pack of cigarettes, and both he and Mrs. Leggett lit up. Whew, the conversation was bad enough without the smoke. Unfortunately, Dr. Leggett was an authority on practically everything. Phyllis raised her eyebrows at me as if we were really in for it. I rolled down my window and leaned my head back to keep from getting carsick.

"Years ago, the metal plates for counterfeiting money had to be hand-engraved and that took real skill. Now, with the offset printing process, if you can take a picture of it, you can print it . . ."

At least Dr. Leggett was off the subject of Dad, but I didn't think I could listen to one more word about counterfeiting. Besides, I was definitely getting carsick. I just hoped it wasn't much farther to Dunbridge High School. I swallowed a couple of times and looked out the window. Trees flashed by in a calendar-picture blur of reds, golds, oranges, browns. For a change, it was a beautiful day, perfect soccer weather, cool with white puffs of mashed-potato clouds in a blue sky.

When we'd arrived from the West Coast, our introduction to New Jersey had been from the New Jersey Turnpike, one depressing stretch of factories, refineries, shopping malls, and sulphury pollution. At least when we got off the highways, the scenery improved. Then, when we hit suburban towns like Fordwick, New Jersey turned out not to be so bad after all.

And country like we were passing through now was even prettier—rolling green hills patchworked by rambling fences. We drove past a herd of grazing brown cows. Before moving to New Jersey I wouldn't have guessed there was a cow in the whole state.

All of a sudden, a big sign just beyond the cow pasture caught my attention. We passed the sign so quickly I had to look out the back window to read it. "H. C. C. C. Service Entrance" was painted on a green sign in yellow letters. An arrow pointed to a long driveway that led up a sloping hill to an enormous brick building perched like a fortress at the top. Smaller outbuildings dotted the hillside.

"What does H. C. C. C. mean?" I interrupted Dr. Leggett in mid-sentence.

"Haven't you been out this way before, Ruth? That's the Harrison County Corrections Center, the county jail."

I stuck my head out the car window just in time to see the big building disappear from view around a bend in the road.

"That jail is over a hundred years old," Dr. Leggett explained. "One of my graduate students teaches high school math to some of the inmates, and he says it's worse on the inside than the out. Most of the . . ."

I didn't hear the rest. H. C. C. C. meant something, but for a minute, I couldn't think what. Then I remembered where I'd seen it. H. C. C. C. had been written in yellow letters on the green van that I'd seen pick up Lou Dargie one day.

·8·
A HEADER

LUCKILY, DUNBRIDGE HIGH SCHOOL wasn't much farther beyond the county jail. We got there just in time. What with the Leggetts' smoking and my shock about the jail, I was ready to throw up. I jumped out of the car and gulped in air. Even so, it wasn't until Phyllis and I found seats at the opposite end of the bleachers from her parents that everything in my throat finally went back down into my stomach where it belonged.

Our seats faced right into the sun, making it hard to see. But I spotted Kenny right away, sitting about five rows in front of us with Paul Sutton. The bleachers weren't exactly jammed. Some Minnisink kids had come, and a lot of parents. Even the Dunbridge side wasn't very crowded, which was too bad because the view was spectacular, like a picture in *National Geographic* titled "Fall." Our Minnisink team wore royal blue shirts and white shorts with matching white knee socks. The Dunbridge uniforms were red and gold.

I wondered if Kenny would turn around and notice us when the opening whistle blew. Everyone jumped to their feet as the soccer ball sailed into the air. Outlined against the blue, blue sky, it twisted and turned as if it were in slow motion. Wham! A Dunbridge player bounced it off his head, and the game had begun. I felt bad when I saw Billy Leggett, Number 15, still sitting on the bench, but maybe he'd get to play later.

Standing up gave me a good chance to study Kenny without his knowing it. He had curlier hair than I had realized, but it was cut short so that his ears showed. They were nice and flat against his head the way I liked. Then he turned to say something to Paul, and I saw his face in profile. Though he had a bump on his nose as if it had been broken, it was a good, strong nose. And his shoulders were broad under his gray sweater. All in all, Kenny looked just as good, if not better, from the back than from the front.

Phyllis nudged me. "There's Kenny Halberstrom."

"Where?" I shaded my eyes and looked all around just as if I hadn't been staring at him.

"Right down there, with Paul Sutton. Hey, Kenny! Paul!" Phyllis waved frantically. My face flushed pink. I just hoped Kenny didn't think it was me as he turned around to see where the shouting had come from. He saw us, waved, then said something to Paul. Paul nodded, and the two of them headed back up the bleacher seats toward us.

I was too embarrassed to do anything but look out at the field. The ball was spinning in the air. A tall, skinny Minnisink player leapt up to head it at the same time as one of the Dunbridge players. They crashed in midair. The spectators groaned as the two players fell to the ground in a tangle of blue and white and red and gold. They rolled over, then were still. The coaches and trainers ran out onto the field as the other players gathered around. Silence. There was not a sound to be heard but the distant scream of a buzz saw. Then the huddle on the field opened, and the two players were on their feet, wobbly, but standing. Everyone clapped as both players were helped back to their benches.

"Hi, Ruth." I jumped. Kenny was right beside me. In the excitement of the collision, I hadn't realized that Kenny and Paul had reached our row.

"Hi." I grinned like an idiot.

"Hey, Kenny, over here." Phyllis leaned across me and signaled Kenny to sit next to her. But Kenny stepped back and sort of pushed Paul ahead of him. So there we were, Phyllis on the end, then Paul, then me, then Kenny. A perfect arrangement.

"How're you doing?" Kenny was grinning too. His eyes were definitely hazel, brown flecked with gold.

"Fine. Really good."

"I was sure those players were really hurt."

"Maybe Minnisink can win today for a change."

We had both spoken at once.

"Go ahead," Kenny said.

"No, you go."

Each of us waited for the other. Then, when neither of us said anything, we burst out laughing, as if it were the funniest thing that had ever happened. Kenny moved closer to me on the bench and pressed his arm against mine. He reached down and took my hand in his.

And that's the way we watched the game, just

sitting, holding hands. Phyllis was jabbering at Paul a mile a minute, but Kenny and I didn't say much of anything. We talked a little about the game, but mostly we just watched, booing or cheering as the ball went first one way, then the other.

Right after half-time, Phyllis reached around Paul and grabbed my arm. Billy Leggett, Number 15, was checking in with the referee as substitute for right wing. His shorts and socks glistened snow white. By now, the other players' uniforms were filthy, splattered with mud, and streaked with grass stains.

"Go, Billy!" That was Dr. Leggett, dignified Dr. Leggett.

The four of us stood up. Right away the ball came to Billy. Just as he got set to kick, it took a little hop and bounced over his foot. He turned to follow the ball, but a Dunbridge player already had it and was dribbling it back up the field. Oh, no, Billy would be taken out of the game before he even got his uniform dirty. But Billy wasn't about to be beat out. He tore down the field, even outrunning his own teammates, got his foot on the ball, and flicked it right past two Dunbridge players. He started back up the field with it, with three Dunbridge players in pursuit.

"Down in front," came a shout from behind. All four of us quickly sat down as Kenny took my hand again.

It was quite a game. Minnisink finally won, and Billy played almost the whole second half. He didn't score, but when the game was over, he looked as dirty and tired as the rest of the team, and even happier. It was a glorious, beautiful day. The only thing that kept it from being perfect was Lou. Every once in a while my mind's eye saw a slide-projector image of that stone fortress of a jail. But I wouldn't let myself think about it. Later. I'd talk to Dad about Lou later.

After the game, the bleachers cleared out fast. I saw Dr. and Mrs. Leggett gather up their things and turn around to look for Phyllis and me.

"I guess I have to go now, Kenny," I said.

He was still holding my hand. "Do you know Jake Belson?"

"Sort of. I know who he is." Wow, this was it.

"He's giving a party next . . ."

"Kenny! Paul! We're waiting!" A high school girl stood on the field, waving up at us. A boy stood beside her with his arm around her waist.

Kenny made a face. "That's my sister. Her boyfriend is our ride home. We gotta go."

"But . . ." I protested.

"Kenny, move it!" Kenny's sister looked mad. She had the same curly brown hair as Kenny, but she didn't look anything like him. She wore lots of make-up and had on really tight jeans. I decided I didn't much like her.

"I'll call you." Kenny squeezed my hand, then dropped it.

"But . . ." I said again.

It was too late. Kenny was already running down the empty bleacher seats two at a time, with Paul behind him.

"We'd better get going too, or Dad will have a fit." Phyllis rolled up her program and stuck it in her pocket. "Wasn't that great to run into Kenny and Paul? I think Paul's cute in a short sort of way, don't you? He was talking about Jake Belson's party. Did Kenny say anything to you about it? Hey, didn't you think Billy played a good game . . ."

Phyllis's voice went on and on as we followed the Leggetts to the parking lot. I didn't listen. My "but" still echoed in my head. Kenny was just about to ask me to Jake Belson's party when his dumb sister butted in. I was sure of it. Now I'd have to wait for him to call.

·9·
A PRIVATE ROOM

ON OUR WAY BACK FROM THE SOCCER GAME, we passed the county jail again which reminded me of Lou. As soon as the Leggetts dropped me home, I pumped Dad. Did he know that Lou was picked up by a van that probably came from the county jail? County jail! Maybe Lou was a prisoner.

That's exactly what he was, Dad said. Ever since we'd moved to Fordwick, Dad had been working with the prisoners at the county jail and had gotten to know Lou especially well. Dad had signed Lou out on a work-release program which meant Lou worked days at St. Martin's and spent his nights in jail.

Lou a criminal! I could hardly believe it. But at least it solved the mystery of what Chief Nussen had meant when he talked about the Lou Dargie setup. The next morning, when Mom and I went to church, I studied Lou. His eyes, I decided, were definitely shifty, and in his black sexton's robes, he looked thinner and paler than ever. Prison pallor was what they called it on TV.

It was hard to concentrate on the church service.

First, I stewed about Lou. Then I started thinking about Kenny. I remembered how warm and strong his hand had been and wondered what it would be like to kiss him. If only his sister hadn't shown up just when he was about to ask me to Jake's party. At least he said he'd call. Maybe tonight.

Mom poked me with her elbow. I snapped to attention. Had I said something out loud? No, it was just that Mom always knew when I wasn't listening in church. I couldn't help it. Daydreaming about Kenny was a lot more interesting than the sermon. We had a guest preacher who used lots of wordy words and gestures, not like Dad, who told jokes to make his point.

I looked around. That's probably why so few people had come to church. They must have heard that Dad wasn't preaching. Besides, it was another beautiful day like yesterday, and people were raking leaves . . . or playing golf . . . or were mixed up about the time because we'd gone off Daylight Savings Time last night . . . or . . . I tried to push the thought to the back of my mind, but it wouldn't stay there . . . or maybe people believed that St. Martin's really was involved in counterfeiting and that Dad had something to do with it.

"A mighty fortress is our God . . ." I jumped up and sang out the final hymn in my usual off-key voice.

After church Dad shook hands with everyone except for Mom, Janice, and me, whom he always kissed. Though I liked it when I was little, now it embarrassed me. One Sunday I'd ducked out a side door, but Dad had been hurt. Since then, I'd just gone through with it.

"Ruth, do you know what day it is tomorrow?" Mrs.

Cole, with Oliver and Lisa, was waiting for me on the church steps.

It's Monday, October . . . uh . . . thirtieth," I guessed.

"Wrong, it's the twenty-ninth," Oliver corrected me.

"It's the last Monday of the month, time to mail out the church newsletter. Can I count on you tomorrow, Ruth?" It wasn't really a question.

Oh no, the last of the month already. Stapling, folding, and stuffing the newsletter into envelopes was the church job I had pledged to do when I was confirmed last year. It was really boring. Every time I did it, I decided to pledge my time to something else, then always forgot until it was too late. Like now.

Monday afternoon, armed with Coke and Fritos, I showed up at the church office. Mrs. Cole, busily typing away, had a table all set up for me with the newsletters, envelopes, and stapler ready and waiting.

I'd been working about an hour when Miss Kunzinger appeared in the office door with a loud sigh. Miss Kunzinger never just walked into a room, she always made an appearance. Miss Kunzinger had been the church organist for twelve years and had lived that whole time on the third floor of the Parish House. She had long, curly red hair and wore dark lipstick and green eyeshadow. She was short and overweight, though I knew she was always on a weird new diet. Dad said she was a brilliant musician, and artists, like Miss Kunzinger, had a special sensitivity that needed pampering. I knew what he meant was, she had a temper. Luckily, he was usually able to kid her out of staying mad.

Miss Kunzinger snapped a yellow piece of paper down on Mrs. Cole's desk. "Here's the list of next

Sunday's hymns for the rector's approval, though why he can't trust my judgment on what hymns to sing like the other rectors of St. Martin's always have, is beyond me. Oh hello there, Ruth dear, are you helping out today?" Miss Kunzinger acted as if she'd just noticed me. It was a phony. She probably counted on me repeating her little dig about the hymns to Dad, which I definitely wouldn't do.

Miss Kunzinger flipped her long red hair over her shoulder and left. Watching her go, I wondered if she dyed her hair. It was red-red hair, and Miss Kunzinger had to be at least forty. I always noticed red hair, because with my fair skin and freckles that's what I'd always thought I should have instead of plain brown.

By 4:30, I was tired, and the palm of my hand ached from pressing the stapler over and over. Mrs. Cole must have been tired, too. She poured herself a cup of coffee and drank it while I finished my second Coke.

"Ruth, do you ever tie your shoelaces or tuck in your blouse?" Mrs. Cole sounded just like Mom.

I blushed. Ever since I'd lost weight with the flu, my shirttails were harder than ever to keep in.

"Can you baby-sit for us Saturday night?" Mrs. Cole asked after I'd fixed myself up.

Saturday night had been on my mind for two days. Kenny hadn't called yet about Jake Belson's party. I had sat by the phone all Sunday night, but the two calls I'd gotten had both been from Phyllis. Then today when I didn't see Kenny in school, I'd checked the absentee list and found his name on it. He must be sick.

So Mrs. Cole asking me to sit Saturday night put me on the spot. I owed the Coles baby-sitting time, but Kenny had said he would call.

"I'm not sure, Mrs. Cole. Can I let you know later?"

"No later than Thursday, please. If you can't sit, I don't want just anyone taking care of Oliver and Lisa."

It was amazing how super-fussy the Coles were about their kids. If they knew how often Oliver conned me, they wouldn't have wanted me to sit either. And what about Lou? Lou had been working at the Coles' every Saturday all fall, painting the trim on their house. I bet the Coles would have a fit if they knew Lou was a prisoner at the county jail.

Mrs. Cole and I had just started back to work when Mr. Edmonds stuck his head in the office door. With his long, thin face, Mr. Edmonds always reminded me of a beardless Abraham Lincoln. I wondered if Abraham Lincoln's feet had been big. For sure, Mr. Edmonds had the biggest feet I'd ever seen, and his hands were big too, all bony and knuckly.

"Where's Lou, Mrs. Cole? I want to clean some leaves out of a gutter and I can't find the ladder."

"Lou has gone for the day, but he was using the ladder over in the nursery school," Mrs. Cole answered.

"Then it's probably still there." Mr. Edmonds sounded irritated. "I left my keys home. May I borrow yours?"

Mrs. Cole opened her desk drawer and gave Mr. Edmonds her ring of keys labeled "Secretary." "Believe me, this place is going to miss that man when he moves to Arizona," she commented when Mr. Edmonds had left. "With his money, he could afford to pay someone to do all the work he does around here. It's a labor of love, that's what it is."

Getting out the newsletter should be a labor of love,

too, but it wasn't. I'd just have to remember to find another church job before the end of next month.

By the time I finally finished, it was 5:30 and dark. Because Mrs. Cole had a few things left to do, I started up the hall by myself, flicking off lights as I went, like Mrs. Cole asked me to. But when I stepped into the Seabury room to turn off the main switch, I noticed the basement door was half-open. The last time I'd come by here, Mr. Edmonds and Lou had been arguing on the basement stairs. All of a sudden, I was curious. I opened the door all the way.

"Hello, is anybody there?" I yelled.

There was no answer, just my voice disappearing down the stairway.

"Hello?" I called again, but again got no answer.

I turned on the stair light and started down. The wooden stairs, so ancient they were worn thin in the middle, led right into the main basement room. It was huge. The concrete floor sloped down to a big center drain, which meant this basement probably leaked like ours at home. A network of pipes and beams crisscrossed overhead, with narrow barred windows set high up in the walls. And of all things, I heard a couple of crickets chirping away. Every damp basement in Fordwick must come complete with crickets.

There was a closed door in front of me and three or four open passageways leading off in other directions. I felt like Alice in Wonderland, not knowing where to start, not even sure I wanted to start at all. It was an awfully big basement, and awfully echoey. But I was here, and there was no way I was about to turn around and go back up without at least taking a look. Well, first things first. I opened the door straight ahead and found myself in the furnace room. A rumbling oil burner and a monster of an oil tank filled the whole space.

I backed out and headed slowly down the first passageway to my right. The five doors opening off it all led into dark and musty rooms crammed with old furniture and desks and bookshelves and garden tools and snow equipment and broken screens and discarded prayer books and hymnals. Most of the rooms were dead ends, but some had crawl spaces that led to I-didn't-know-where, and I-wasn't-about-to-find-out. In the whole basement, only one door was locked, the Bellows Room door. Last summer some kids had gotten into the Bellows Room and slashed the leather bellows of the organ. There was such an uproar about it, the Bellows Room had been locked ever since.

All in all, it was disappointing. It was just a giant basement-type basement like the one in our house, only crammed with more junk. Then, as I started back toward the main basement room, I passed a little recess in the wall leading to a closed door I hadn't noticed before. Since it was the only room I hadn't checked out, I decided to take a look. But just as I reached for the doorknob, I felt a sneeze coming on. Oh, no, not flu again. I pulled a Kleenex out of my slicker pocket. Everything else in my pocket came out with it, coins, dust balls, tardy notices, hall passes, Chapstick, pencil stubs. They scattered all over the floor. I sneezed and blew my nose. Maybe it's just the dust and cobwebs and not the flu, I hoped, as I quickly picked everything up, stuffed it all back in my pocket, and pushed open the door.

When I turned on the light, I realized right away I

was in Lou's room. His Sunday sexton's robe hung on a hook, and an ash tray overflowed with cigarette butts. There wasn't much else in the room, just a beat-up chair, a table, a lamp, and a pile of old magazines. An out-of-date calendar hung on the wall next to a mirror, and a pair of shiny black shoes stuck out from under the chair. Something else stuck out too. It was a long, black cord with a strange-looking plug on the end of it. I pulled on the cord. Something heavy and familiar slid out. A telephone.

What a strange place for a phone, especially since it wasn't even plugged in. But there, on the floorboard, was an outlet with four holes that just fit the four prongs on the plug. I connected them. When I lifted the receiver, I heard a dial tone. Its loud buzzing startled me. What if the phone started ringing? I had to be crazy, messing around in Lou's room. I pulled out the plug, shoved the phone back under the chair, and ran. This basement wasn't just full of junk, it was spooky, that's what it was. More than spooky, plain scary.

I had just closed Lou's door behind me when I heard a tap-tap on the basement stairs. I paused, my eyes wide open as if that would help me hear better. It sounded like footsteps. It *was* footsteps. Someone was coming down the stairs. I was still out of sight in the little alcove so I couldn't see who it was, and whoever it was, couldn't see me. I mustn't move. Maybe they'd go away.

Then I went weak with relief. Mrs. Cole must have seen the light on and come down to check. I started to call out, then stopped. Mrs. Cole would have shouted down the stairway first, just as I had.

The footsteps had almost reached the bottom of the

stairs, and for sure it wasn't the sound of Mrs. Cole's spike-heeled shoes. It was a man's heavy tread. I froze, with my fist pressed to my mouth. I couldn't scream, or make a sound. I just couldn't. It might be Lou. Maybe he hadn't left after all. Maybe he'd been hiding and seen me snooping in his room. He might kill me. What if he were already in jail for murder?

My throat squeezed so tight, I couldn't have screamed if I had wanted to. Lou could kill me down here and no one would know. Black headlines blazed out at me. "Rector's Daughter Disappears." Kenny would read it and know that Dad was a minister. It didn't matter. It would be too late for me to care.

·10·
PLAYROOM SECRET

THE FOOTSTEPS STOPPED. They had reached the bottom of the stairs. In the silence, all I could hear was the throb of the furnace, the cricket duet, and my strangled breath wheezing in and out. The footsteps moved again, but it was impossible to tell in which direction.

Then I remembered the phone in Lou's room. I could use it to call home . . . or the police. I started to edge back toward the door. My palms were sweaty as they slid along the cold cinder-block wall. But in the few steps it took me to reach Lou's room, I knew it wouldn't work. The door was shut. I couldn't open it without being heard. Not only that, but what if Lou was headed for his room? I sagged against the wall. It was hopeless.

"Ruth!"

Even before I spun around, my mind registered that the voice was much deeper than Lou's. But I was too paralyzed to recognize the tall shadowy figure.

"Ruth Saunders, what are you doing here?" It was Mr. Edmonds, and he held a big monkey wrench in one hand like a weapon.

"I ... I ... was just looking around ..." I could hardly talk.

"I knew Mrs. Cole was still in her office so when I saw the lights on down here, I thought you were a prowler. I could have killed you." Mr. Edmonds lowered his arm. He looked shaken himself. Then he nodded toward Lou's door. "That room's off limits. You haven't been in there, have you?"

"I've never been in the church basement before, Mr. Edmonds. I was just looking around." My throat was still too dry to talk right.

"And scaring the wits out of me. Come on, you'd better be getting home." For such a big man, Mr. Edmonds' grip was gentle as he took my arm and steered me toward the stairs.

I was glad he had hold of me. Knees really could turn to rubber, and that's what had happened to mine. I hardly had the strength to get up the stairs.

That night, for the first time in weeks, Dad asked me to play backgammon after dinner. But I didn't do much better than I had the first time I played. I just couldn't concentrate. Every time the phone rang, I jumped up to answer, sure it was, hopefully, Kenny, or hopefully not, Mr. Edmonds, calling to tell Dad how he'd found me snooping around the church basement. But none of the calls concerned me. They were either for Mom, or business for Dad.

As the week went by and Dad didn't mention my basement adventure, I worried less about Mr. Edmonds telling on me, and more about Kenny. He was absent both Monday and Tuesday, so I figured he was sick, maybe with flu like I'd had. Then on Wednesday I spotted him eating lunch by himself in the cafeteria. Good. It was the perfect chance for him to ask me to Jake Belson's party. I grabbed a carton of milk and a roll and raced over to his table.

"Hi, Kenny, how are you? Have you been sick?" I slid into the seat next to his. He certainly looked sick, grayish-pale and tired.

Surprisingly, he blushed and looked down at his tray, stirring his stew around with his fork. "Oh, hi," he mumbled. "Ah, yeah, I was sick, I guess."

"Maybe it was flu like I had." I opened my lunch bag and pulled out celery sticks, raw carrots, a protein-bread sandwich, and a bunch of grapes. Mom had me on another diet. I shoved everything back and buttered my roll.

"Yeah, that must be it, the flu." Kenny still hadn't looked at me.

All of a sudden I couldn't think of anything to say. "That was a good game last Saturday, don't you think?" I blurted out.

"Yeah, I guess so." Kenny pushed back his tray. He'd hardly eaten anything. "Well, I gotta go now. See ya."

And just like that he was gone. At the soccer game he'd been ready to ask me to Jake Belson's party. I know he had. Now he wouldn't even look at me. In a state of shock, I stared at the cafeteria door as Kenny disappeared out it.

That night Phyllis and I discussed the situation on the phone. The only answer we could come up with was that Kenny had found out that Dad was a minister, and it had really turned him off. Well, if that was his reason, I told Phyllis, I'd cross him off my list, too. That was easy to say but not so easy to do. For the next few days, every time the phone rang, I ran for it, hoping against hope it was Kenny. It never was. Then to top off a rotten week, Paul Sutton asked Phyllis to go to Jake's party with him. Paul was at least four inches shorter than Phyllis, but all of a sudden Phyllis decided it was immature to let height make a difference in a relationship.

From then on Phyllis had me crazy. Should she wear a dress or blue jeans, stockings or socks, dress shoes or flats? Should she blow-dry her hair or roll it in curlers? What about jewelry, a chain necklace, or her locket? She called me a minimum of twice a night to go over what we'd already decided during the day. At least she was too excited about the party to ask me about the Band raffle tickets. I'd lost them somewhere before I'd sold a one.

Then it was Saturday night. Kenny had never called, and no fairy godmother had waved a wand over my head like Cinderella and whisked me away to the party. All I had to look forward to was baby-sitting for Oliver and Lisa.

Surprisingly, Mr. Cole was wearing a tuxedo when he picked me up in his new gray Mercedes Saturday night. With his Coke-bottle glasses and black, black hair, Mr. Cole wasn't exactly handsome, but all dressed up, I had to admit he looked pretty good. But Mrs. Cole was the one who really surprised me. She had on a burgundy velvet jump suit with a plunging neckline, lots of clunky gold jewelry, and no eye glasses. She must have been wearing contact lenses. I had to be in the wrong house.

"Hello, Mrs. Cole," I managed to get out.

"Good evening, Ruth. Oliver and Lisa are down in the playroom. I've left our phone number on the bulletin board as well as the police, fire department, doctor, and First Aid Squad numbers. We'll be home by midnight. Now you be sure to call if anything comes up."

I wasn't in the wrong house after all. It was just that Cinderella's fairy godmother had waved her wand over Mrs. Cole instead of me.

As soon as I went down to the basement, Kenny and Jake Belson's party went right out of my head. The playroom was a disaster. Oliver and Lisa were playing golf through an obstacle course of chairs and tables and stacked-up books. The water hole, a pie plate full of water, had already spilled and needed mopping up. But Oliver and Lisa were tired of golf. Though we tried Ping-Pong, Lisa cried every time she missed the ball, which was more than she hit it. Dominoes, Pick-Up Sticks, and building with the Lego set didn't last much longer. Then, while Lisa and I were playing with her doll house, Oliver put a big hole in a lampshade with one of his father's golf clubs.

Not only did I forget my problems, I forgot the time. I got Oliver and Lisa to bed an hour late, and it was an hour after that before they settled down. They called me back about six times, to find Lisa's blankie, turn on the night light, get Oliver a drink of water, take Lisa to the bathroom. Mrs. Cole had said she didn't want just anyone to sit for Oliver and Lisa. I didn't think just anyone could do it, and that included me.

I was beat as I collapsed on the sofa to watch TV. And hungry. I wished the Coles had some decent junk food in the house. It would pick me up. As it was, I felt myself dozing off.

I woke with a start. The eleven o'clock news was almost over. The Coles were due back at twelve, and the playroom was a wreck. I raced down into the basement. I had just crawled under the Ping-Pong table to pick up Legos, when the phone rang. It startled me so, I jumped, cracking my head on the underside of the table. Shaken, I crawled on my hands and knees to the phone. Mrs. Cole was probably calling to check on the kids.

"Hello, Coles' residence." I tried to sound alert.

"Is that you, Ruth?" asked a whispery little voice that was hard to hear over a background of music and loud voices.

"Yes, this is Ruth. Who is this?"

"It's me, you idiot, Phyllis. I'm at the party."

Great. Here I'd been knocking myself out all night, and Phyllis was calling to gloat. At least I could find out about Kenny. "Is Kenny there?"

"No." Phyllis was still whispering. "It's wild."

Relieved about Kenny, I stretched out the long phone cord and kept on picking up Legos. "So what's happening?"

"There aren't any parents here, just Jake's older brother and his high school friends. They're drinking beer and getting drunk. It's like an orgy. Paul's father was supposed to pick us up at eleven, but he never came. I don't know what to do."

It finally dawned on me. Phyllis was whispering because she was scared. "I thought your mother called the Belsons and checked the party out."

"Mrs. Belson said there'd be a responsible adult at

the party. She must have meant the maid. The maid was here for a while, then went to bed." Phyllis sounded close to tears.

"Why don't you call your father to come get you?"

"If he saw what was going on he'd never let me leave the house again. Half the kids are in the living room making out."

And I'd been jealous. Wow, was I glad Kenny wasn't there, making out with some eighth-grade girl.

"What'll I do?" Phyllis started crying.

"Call a taxi." The idea came to me like a lightning flash of genius.

"Yeaah." Phyllis breathed the word out. "There're three of us here who have to get home. We can split the cost."

Phyllis hung up without even saying good-bye. I didn't care. Missing that party was the only good thing that had happened to me all week. With a sudden spurt of energy, I finished straightening up.

There, except for the torn lampshade, the room looked pretty good. All that were left were the piles of dominoes, Pick-Up Sticks and Legos. Maybe there were some boxes in the closet by the bar. Sure enough, the empty boxes were on the top shelf. I started to reach for them, then stopped. The whole floor of the closet was stacked with rolls of paper wrapped in plastic. Though they were about the size of paper-towel rolls, that's not what they were. "Crane 100% Rag Paper" was written on the wrappers in red script. I stared at the writing. It rang a bell somewhere . . . one hundred percent rag paper. . . .

Dr. Leggett, that's where. I remembered that counterfeit money lecture he'd given Phyllis and me on our way to the soccer game. He'd said something about how the Treasury Department used one hundred percent rag paper for printing money.

I picked up one of the rolls, unwrapped the plastic, and pulled out a length of the white paper. It was crinkly and crisp, the same paper I'd seen on Mr. Cole's desk the last time I'd baby-sat, the notepaper I'd doodled on. At the time, I'd compared it to my ten-dollar bill, then forgotten all about it, because the notepaper didn't have any squiggly lines in it like the money. But Dr. Leggett had said something else about printing counterfeit money. I tried to remember. Hadn't he said the counterfeiters couldn't copy the colored lines, so they had to make do with plain paper, paper like this?

I counted the rolls. There were eight. It was certainly enough paper to make as much counterfeit money as anyone would need. Lots and lots of money. And that's certainly what the Coles seemed to have plenty of lately. Dad had said Mr. Cole had a good new job, but I didn't see how any new job could pay for everything the Coles had done this fall, painting and decorating their whole house, joining the Country Club, private schools for the kids, a new Mercedes. Not only that, but one of my ten dollar ski-trip bills had been baby-sitting money the Coles had paid me.

·11·
AN OFFICE VISITOR

I WASN'T THINKING ABOUT MUCH OF ANY-THING as Phyllis and I bumped along in the school bus the following Monday. It was a cold and rainy day that just fit my bad mood. I was in more than a bad mood, I was depressed. I had convinced myself that Kenny hadn't wanted to go to Jake Belson's party, or that maybe his parents wouldn't let him go, but now that the party was over, Kenny was still avoiding me. In school today, when I'd smiled and waved as we passed in the hall, he'd pretended not to see me.

Phyllis was silent too. She was still pretty shook up about Saturday night. When she'd arrived home an hour past her deadline, in a taxi, her parents had been so furious they had grounded her for a week.

I leaned my head against the closed bus window. Ernestine, the driver, and some of the kids were smoking, and I had a headache. The bus lurched to a stop a block up from St. Martin's, the stop before mine. I was watching the rain weep down the dirty bus window, when I realized something was going on across the street at St. Martin's.

A gray car was parked on the grass by one of the church's rear doors, a door that was never used as far as I knew. I recognized the car right away. It was the Coles' new Mercedes. A man was bent over the car trunk. He straightened up, holding something in his arms covered with a poncho against the rain. It was Lou.

Ernestine shifted and we slowly started up again. As we passed the church, I got a better view. It looked like . . . it certainly looked like the car trunk was filled with rolls of paper wrapped in plastic. But I couldn't be sure. The Mercedes was a good seventy-five yards away.

Then we made a turn onto Wyndham Road, and Lou and the Mercedes were out of sight. I knew I'd seen Lou and I knew I'd seen the Mercedes, but had I seen those rolls of paper? I wasn't sure. Oliver had told me that Lou was painting the trim on their house both Saturday and Sunday afternoons. Maybe Mr. Cole had asked Lou to deliver the rolls of paper to the church . . . except that Lou practically refused to take orders from anyone but Dad . . . and Dad certainly had no use for all that strange, crinkly paper.

When I had told Dad about finding the rolls of paper in the Coles' basement, he had just given me another lecture on snooping around where I didn't belong. Then he had explained that Mr. Cole's new firm handled all sorts of quality paper for engineering uses, and that's all there was to it. Maybe that's all there was to it, I thought as Ernestine drove the bus up Wyndham Road, and maybe not. If the paper was used only for business, why would Mr. Cole have it in his house anyway?

The bus lurched to a stop. Phyllis and I said good-bye, and I ran home alone through the rain. Because I already knew that Mom was working at the Yarn Barn today, I found the key under the window ledge and let myself in. Now that people were beginning to knit and needlepoint presents for Christmas, Mom had been working almost full time lately, like she wanted. Only right now, with less than two weeks to go before the wedding, she wasn't exactly overjoyed with the extra pressure.

I hated an empty house, especially on a dismal day like this. I was lucky I had Tippy. He raised his head and gave one short bark of welcome, then flopped back in his favorite position, with his legs tucked under the radiator. I dropped my wet slicker on the floor and snuggled down beside him.

"What do you think, you adorable little Tippy?" I laid my head on his back. Tippy's long tail thumped with pleasure. Dad said Tippy had the only tail in the world that wagged the dog. From his insides, I heard rumblings and wheezings that sounded like our ancient freezer in the basement.

"I'll tell you what I think, Tip. I think I ought to check out what Lou was unloading from the Coles' car into the church." It certainly beat sitting around all afternoon watching TV and getting more depressed about Kenny.

Tippy wasn't interested. He wriggled out from under me, sat up, and started to scratch. Fine white dog hairs flew all over. Poor Tippy had dry skin. Mom said his everlasting scratching drove her crazy, but

Mom had dry skin herself, so I didn't see how she could complain.

When I ate an order of French Fries at lunch, I had told myself I wouldn't eat after school. But I knew a plate of cold spaghetti would help my headache. I made sure I rinsed off the dirty plate carefully before putting it in the dishwasher. I didn't want to leave any evidence for Mom to nag me about. I put my slicker back on and ran down the hill to St. Martin's.

Oh-oh, Dad's car was in the church parking lot. I'd have to be careful he didn't catch me poking around. I stuck my head around the rear corner of the building. It was still raining and the low back area was marshy. Both Lou and the Mercedes were gone. Deep tire tracks in the muddy grass led out to the street.

I jumped over the puddles and tried to open the church door. Though the ivy around the door frame had been ripped off where Lou had opened it, the door was locked. I peered through the windowed top half and got a big surprise. The door opened onto a staircase. I'd explored St. Martin's pretty carefully, but I'd never seen this staircase before. Lou must have carried those rolls of paper from the Mercedes down these stairs into the basement.

I slopped through the puddles around to the Choir Room door. It was open. I peeked in, thankful it was Monday, and everything was quiet. The room was empty. No Dad, and no Miss Kunzinger either. I ran through the choir room, through the Seabury Room, and over to the basement stairway door. Remembering how Mr. Edmonds had scared me last time, I decided not to turn on any lights until I was safely at the bottom.

I pulled the door shut behind me and started down the stairs. In the pitch dark, I had to hold onto the railing and feel my way down, one foot at a time. I stopped halfway down and listened. I didn't hear anything. A few more steps. Stop. Listen. Still nothing.

But wait. I wrinkled my nose. There *was* something. Cigarette smoke. Then I heard a muffled voice talking. Lou. It was Lou's cigarette smoke and Lou's voice! Someone else, not Lou, must have driven the Mercedes back to the Coles'. I grabbed the railing with both hands to steady myself as I turned and started back up the stairs with slow-motion care.

Wait a minute. There was something strange about Lou's voice. He said a few words, paused, then said a few more. But no one was answering. Of course, Lou was talking on his telephone. And if Lou were on the phone, there was no way for him to know I was listening. I snuck back down a few stairs. I didn't stop to think whether what I was doing was right or wrong. I just knew I had to find out what Lou was up to. He might even be calling someone about those rolls of paper. I crept all the way down to the bottom step.

"I want twelve on Golden Dancer in the fifth . . . ten on Misty Prince in the sixth . . . twelve on Tony's Girl in the seventh . . ." Lou was reciting lists of numbers and strange names like some kind of code. I listened for something understandable, but it was all numbers and funny names. "Awright, I'll be in touch." Lou clicked the phone down.

I'd better get out of here. I took the stairs two at a time. When I reached the Seabury Room, I was panting like I'd just finished the Boston marathon. I was sweaty hot under my slicker, and my headache was back. I had to do something, but what? Dad. Lou was Dad's project, let Dad handle it. He'd have a fit when he heard I'd been in the church basement, but I had to take the chance. Lou was up to something weird that Dad ought to know about.

I raced down the hall past Mrs. Cole's office. It was empty. She must have driven the Mercedes home herself. I knocked on Dad's closed door.

"Come in," he called.

I started talking before I even got in the room. "Dad, Lou is in the . . ." I stopped short. Bishop Bayley, complete with purple vest and gold cross, sat opposite Dad's desk.

He stood right up and gave me a hug, wet slicker and all. Bishop Bayley was a big man, with lots of gray hair and a reddish tan face that always looked like he'd just played golf. Though he was Janice's godfather, I had never known him very well. He pulled out a chair for me next to his. "Ruthie, dear, what a treat to see you. I want to hear everything you've been doing. How do you like New Jersey? What about school? Have you made friends?"

Because he sounded like he really wanted to know, I started to tell him . . . school was okay, and New Jersey was okay, too. . . . But Dad interrupted.

"Gordon and I have business to discuss, Ruthie. Tell me what you have on your mind, then skoot along."

Skoot along. He made me sound like I was seven. Then I registered on what Dad had asked. But I didn't want to discuss Lou in front of the bishop.

Dad saw me hesitate. "Gordon's an old friend, Ruthie, and quite unshockable. Now what is it?"

No matter what Dad said, I couldn't look at either

Dad or Bishop Bayley as I told them how I'd overheard Lou on his phone talking in some kind of code with numbers and crazy names like Golden Dancer and Tony's Girl. I decided not to even mention Lou unloading what looked like counterfeit money paper into the church basement. Enough honesty was enough.

Actually, I expected Dad to be furious about me snooping around the church after he'd forbidden it, but to my surprise, he didn't even mention it. Instead, he stared at Bishop Bayley with a stunned look, and Bishop Bayley stared back. The bishop spoke first. "It sounds like St. Martin's has gone in for a little off-track betting on the horses, Henry."

"I can't believe it . . ." Dad locked and unlocked his fingers. "How do you suppose he rigged up the phone?"

Bishop Bayley leaned forward in his chair. "This is your prisoner from the Corrections Center?"

Dad nodded. "Lou Dargie is a good man. I must admit this takes me by surprise, but I'll put a stop to it fast, believe me."

"Have you checked into this work-release program carefully? They've had some trouble with it on the state level."

I had no idea what they were talking about, but they seemed to have forgotten me, and I wasn't about to leave until they told me to.

"Warden McKenzie is doing a fine job, Gordon. I can testify to that," Dad said. "Of course, there's always some risk in a program like this, but anything worth doing is a risk. No, I won't back down on this program. It's all the hope men like Lou Dargie have."

"Well, you've read this new batch of letters I've

received from your parishioners." Bishop Bayley tapped a pile of letters on Dad's desk. "I'm not sure I like the tone of them, Henry, and I don't mean your hiring Florence Atkins as your assistant. I'll back you all the way on that. What concerns me is a feeling of uneasiness . . . restlessness . . . call it what you want, but I'm hearing altogether too much about these instances St. Martin's has had with counterfeiting. Whether the grievances are valid or not, Henry, it's got to be cleared up. This sort of thing can seriously hurt a church."

Dad reached over, picked up the stack of letters, and handed them back to the bishop. "I'll take care of Lou immediately. As to the rest, I'm sorry that it puts you on the spot, Gordon. Just give me a couple of weeks to straighten it out, let's say, until after Janice's wedding. Then if you're not satisfied with the way things are going, you can step in any way you want. I'll even resign if you think that's what's best for the church."

All of a sudden, I didn't want to hear any more. I didn't understand everything, but I certainly understood the word "resign." And good friend or not, Bishop Bayley looked really annoyed.

·12·
A BACKGAMMON GAME

I'D ALWAYS COMPLAINED ABOUT DAD'S JOB, but the thought of his resigning made me feel terrible. And if Dad worried about money now, it would be a hundred times worse if he didn't have a job. Besides, I knew he loved being a minister; and because he liked people and people liked him, I knew he was good at it, too. To cheer Dad up, I resolved to be helpful, responsible, and pleasant.

And to cheer myself up, I resolved to do something positive about Kenny. Now. Right away. Tomorrow.

The very next day I forced myself to wait outside the boys' locker room, knowing that when Kenny finished gym, he had history at the other end of the building. We could walk along the hall together. I didn't know what I'd say to him, but I was counting on something brilliant just popping into my head.

Kenny seemed really surprised to see me standing there by the locker room door. But even blushing, he looked handsome, with his wet hair all slicked back from the shower.

"Hi, Kenny."

"Hi." He looked away and walked quickly past me.

I turned and caught up to him, clutching my books to my chest so tight they practically cut into my ribs. "Are you going to the high school soccer game on Saturday?" which was the brilliant remark I came up with.

"I dunno. Maybe." Kenny was walking faster and faster. The halls were crowded, and I kept bumping into people as I hurried to catch up.

"Probably now that Billy played so much last time, the Leggetts will be going to every game, so that means I'll be going too . . ."

Kenny didn't answer. He just nodded.

"Ah . . . well, maybe I'll see you there." I laughed, but it sounded fake, even to me. Why hadn't I planned out what I wanted to say!

"I'm going in here. So long."

With a fast turn to his left, Kenny practically ran into the boys' room. The door swung shut in my face.

And that was that.

The Kenny-situation was bad enough, but on Wednesday, a ninth-grade boy got called into the school office, just as I had, and word was that he'd passed a bad ten dollar bill in the cafeteria. Though I didn't know the boy, I unfortunately knew who he was. He and his family were members of St. Martin's, and his father was head usher.

Those weren't the only disasters of the week. On Thursday, my Damson Plum bridesmaid dress arrived, and it didn't fit. There was enough material in the bust to wrap around me twice, padded bra or no padded bra. With only a week and a half to go before the wedding, Mom and I rushed it back to Olga's Bridal

Shoppe for alterations. Even Olga laughed when she saw me in it.

If things weren't working out for me, they were working out worse for Dad. The same day as my too-big bridesmaid's dress arrived, everyone on the church mailing list got a letter. Phyllis snitched her parents' and showed it to me. I wished she hadn't. It was all about how Episcopalians must stand by their traditions and not let the new prayer book and the new worship service and especially, women priests, ruin the church. There was a whole paragraph about counterfeit money and how, coincidentally, more of it seemed to show up at St. Martin's than anywhere else. Though Dad's name wasn't mentioned, the meaning was clear, that Dad was the one responsible for what was going on at the church.

It was a terrible blow. Letters to the bishop were bad enough, but this letter had gone out to everyone in the church. I read it again. It sounded just as awful the second time as it had the first. And it was printed on yellow paper, a perfect color, because whoever wrote it, had been too chicken to sign it. Dad always said that anything not signed, wasn't worth reading. Maybe everyone felt that way. I hoped so, but I doubted it. The strange part was, the letter was printed on the same yellow paper the church used for the Newsletter. I crumpled it up and threw it away, forgetting it wasn't even mine to get rid of. I just hoped Mom and Dad never saw it.

That night I had just gotten into bed and was reading *Johnny Tremain* for English, when there was a knock on my door.

"Ruthie, may I come in?"

It was Dad, with his backgammon board under his

arm. He sat down on my bed, opened the board, and set up the men. He didn't say a word. He just rolled the dice to see who would go first. I didn't say anything either. I smoothed the covers on my bed to make it flat and took my turn with the dice. I rolled a double six. Nothing had changed. Everything was still a mess, but I just knew that double six was good luck. We'd work things out somehow, Dad and I together.

We played the whole game in silence, except for saying "good move," or "your turn," or "how dare you bump my man?" When we had finished a close game, which Dad won, he folded up the board and moved nearer to me on the bed. The mattress squeaked under his weight. He didn't say anything for a minute, as if he were trying to sort out his thoughts. While I waited, I watched the passing cars beam their headlights over my ceiling like a lighthouse sending out signals.

"A couple of things have been on my mind, Ruthie, and I think we ought to have them out," Dad finally said. "I'm sorry you heard Gordon Bayley and me talk so frankly in my office the other day. Neither of us showed good sense, and I apologize. However, I think you owe me an apology as well. I told you not to get involved in any of this business, and you disobeyed me by deliberately eavesdropping on Lou."

"I know, Dad, and I'm sorry."

Dad reached for my hand and traced around each of my fingers the way he used to when I was little. "Lou and I have come to terms on this, and together we disconnected his phone. Lou's betting is over, and as far as you're concerned, it never happened. I don't want you to discuss this with Phyllis or anyone else." Dad smiled at me, but I noticed how tired he looked.

"I wouldn't, Dad," I said. "But what's going to

happen about your job?"

"It will work out in time, Ruthie. A new rector always brings change to a church, and change isn't always welcome. The few complainers want to be heard, and at the moment they're pretty vocal. But, Ruthie, you should understand that they're a very small minority, and most of the people are caring and concerned."

Dad knew about the yellow letters. I was as sure of that as if he had told me. I had thought of asking Dad for advice about Kenny, but right now Dad had enough hassle without me dumping on him, too.

He smiled again. "There is absolutely no reason in the world for you to get upset about this, Baby. It isn't anything I can't handle, I promise. Besides, right now you shouldn't have a thing on your mind but the wedding. After all, how many twelve-year-old girls have the privilege of being a full-fledged bridesmaid?"

Hot tears filled my eyes. Dad was hurting, I knew that, and I wanted to help, if only he'd let me. He just didn't realize that I wasn't his Baby anymore, that I was growing up. I wished I could tell him, but my voice didn't work very well.

"Good night, Dad. I love you," was all I could get out.

"And I love you." Dad sounded choked up, too.

·13·
GRAVESIDE

IT WAS FRIDAY AT LAST. What a relief to be out of school for two whole days. And, as an extra dividend, when I got off the school bus, Mom greeted me at the door with a big hug. It was the first afternoon she hadn't worked at the Yarn Barn in over a week.

"Ruthie, I've missed terribly not being here when you get home from school. Your father called and wants to see you in his office, but how about some apple brown betty first?"

"With hard sauce?"

"With hard sauce."

Mom dished up my brown betty, then joined me at the table with a cup of coffee. "School's going all right?" she asked.

"It's okay."

"How about that nice Kenny I met? Do you ever see Kenny in school?"

So that was it. Mom was trying to figure out what

was wrong with me, like Dad had. My attempts to be pleasant must not have been very successful. But I didn't want to talk about Kenny. It was something I had to work out for myself.

"I see Kenny once in a while." I answered without going into detail.

Mom was great. She didn't press. She just drank her coffee and told funny stories about the Yarn Barn.

"Well, you'd better get going, Ruthie," she said, when I was finished. "Your father sounded anxious to see you."

That was strange. When our school bus had passed the church, I'd noticed funeral limousines in the parking lot and figured a funeral was going on. Sure enough, as I walked down Wyndham Drive, I saw the limousines were still there. It was certainly a funeral kind of day, with gray, fast-moving clouds, and a wind that whipped the dry, fall leaves into gusty circles. I ran around to the side and used the Choir Room entrance.

It took my eyes a moment to adjust to the dark Choir Room. As the shadows came into focus, I was surprised to see two figures standing by the far window. Right away I recognized Miss Kunzinger's bright orangy-red hair. She stood behind the curtain peering out the window into the courtyard. Someone in a yellow Altar Guild smock was behind the opposite curtain, looking out the window, too. Then, the person turned her head and the light from outside profiled her beaky nose and stiff black hair. It was Mrs. Moorehead.

". . . sit up and take notice of those . . ." she was saying.

There was no way I was going to get caught eavesdropping again. I cleared my throat and clumped across the Choir Room. Both women jumped and turned around. They seemed so startled to see me, I was sure they had been talking about the church.

Mrs. Moorehead covered up fast. "Hello there, Ruth. I'm on Altar Guild duty, so I'm waiting for your father to finish." She was as cool as if she'd been discussing the weather.

"Hello," I mumbled, not very politely. "Dad wanted me to . . ." My words trailed off. On top of the piano, half-hidden between two stacks of hymn books, was a pile of yellow papers.

Wow, I bet it was some of those unsigned letters. I craned my neck to check if there was printing on the top sheet, but I couldn't see over the pile of hymnals. It would be just like Mrs. Moorehead and Miss Kunzinger to have written that letter and mailed it out to everyone. They'd probably both be happy to see Dad leave St. Martin's forever. And I remembered what a big letter-writer Mrs. Moorehead was to our town newspaper.

"Are you looking for something?" Miss Kunzinger's voice was sharp.

They were both watching me. I blushed furiously, hating myself for it as I shook my head and kept on going through the Choir Room, out into the hall, and into Mrs. Cole's office. I stopped short. Mrs. Cole and Mr. Edmonds were hiding behind the curtains looking out into the courtyard just like Mrs. Moorehead and Miss Kunzinger had been. What was going on around here? It was as if everyone were playing some kind of game I didn't know about. Then I almost laughed out loud. From the back, Mr. Edmonds, in his green windbreaker and green cap, looked just like a spindly, long-legged praying mantis.

"Dad wanted to see me," I announced.

Mrs. Cole started. "Oh, it's you, Ruth. You'll have to wait. The interment isn't over yet."

Was I dumb. No one was playing games. They were all watching Dad bury ashes out in the columbarium. Little mice feet ran up my back. Half of me wanted to see what was going on, and half of me didn't. The curious half won. Slowly, I walked over to the window, pulled back the curtain, and peeked.

The courtyard looked like a Frankenstein movie set. In black and white. A few faded-yellow chrysanthemums in the border garden were the only patch of color. Even the sky was bleakly gray, as if it were about to rain, or maybe snow. Dad stood by a hole in the ground where a flagstone had been removed. About twenty people, mostly gray-haired and old and dressed in black, gathered around him with their heads bowed. Dad's long black cape swirled and fluttered in the wind like flapping crow's wings. And there it was. The urn. I thought a burial urn would be some kind of vase, but it was just a gray metal box, about the size of a shoe box. I wouldn't have guessed there were that many ashes after a cremation.

"Whose funeral is it, Mrs. Cole?"

Mrs. Cole blinked fast three or four times, as if her new contact lenses bothered her. "Mrs. Weemer," she answered.

That was too bad. Mrs. Weemer was a nice old lady. It was also a surprise. Mrs. Weemer was so ancient, she was all bent over and shrunk up. It was hard to believe anyone so tiny would have so many ashes.

Outside, Dad made the sign of the cross in benediction. Mr. Edmonds let the curtain drop. "As soon as everyone leaves, I'll replace the flagstone. I'm due at the dentist at four."

Mrs. Cole was already typing away at her desk. "With the amount of time you put in around here, Mr. Edmonds, you should be paid. I mean it."

"Spare me a higher tax bracket, please. Sometimes I think I work full-time for the government as it is," Mr. Edmonds grumbled as he zipped up his jacket and left the office.

Now the group outside was breaking up and leaving by a side door. As soon as everyone was gone, I saw Mr. Edmonds hurry across the courtyard with long strides. As he bent over to replace the flagstone, I thought again how much he looked like a praying mantis, all stiff angles and awkwardness.

Mr. Edmonds had already finished and left the courtyard by the time Dad stuck his head in Mrs. Cole's office and signaled me with a curt nod to follow him. He seemed angry, as if I'd done something wrong. But that wasn't possible. I'd really worked hard this week to be helpful, responsible, and pleasant. I'd even remembered to tie my shoelaces and keep my shirttails tucked in. Puzzled, I followed Dad into his office.

Dad closed the door, hung up his cape, and slumped into his desk chair. He looked beat, and the thatch of hair that framed his bald spot was all mussed up from the wind, making it seem thinner and grayer than ever.

"Ruthie, did you go and tell Phyllis about Lou's betting?"

I blushed in spite of myself, knowing it made me look

guilty. But it was a blush of anger, not guilt. "Of course I didn't, Dad. How can you think that?"

Dad reached for his candy jar, took out a sourball. and started to suck on it. "I just got back from the Corrections Center. Warden McKenzie got a call this morning about Lou Dargie's betting and he's furious. Even though I explained it's no longer a problem, he's pulled Lou out of the work-release program."

A wave of relief rushed over me. Lou was gone and I was glad. I'd baby-sat for the Coles Thursday afternoon and checked their basement closet for those rolls of paper. They weren't there. It was all the proof I needed to convince me that that was what Lou had been unloading from the Coles' Mercedes into the church basement. I didn't know who ordered Lou to do it, or whether he did it on his own, but now it didn't matter. I didn't care if I never saw Lou again.

Dad went on. "And I'm on the spot for not reporting it in the first place."

But how could that be? Dad hadn't done anything but try to help Lou. What a mess someone had stirred up. "Who called the warden, Dad?"

Dad shrugged his shoulders. "It was anonymous, what else? At first I thought you'd said something to Phyllis and word had gotten out from there. But, of course, you didn't. I see that now. I'm sorry I jumped to conclusions, Baby, but it was a terrible blow."

It was a blow all right. "Anonymous" must mean no-name, like those yellow letters. It seemed to me a no-name phone call was as chicken as an unsigned letter.

"Maybe Bishop Bayley said something, Dad. He heard me tell you about Lou."

Dad stood up and started to pace his office. "No, whoever called the warden called Gordon Bayley at the same time. Gordon phoned me right away, and he was very unhappy about it." Dad stopped pacing and pounded his fist on his desk. "I will not be intimidated on this. I believe Lou is a person of worth, and I won't let him go down the drain."

Dad's concern for Lou made me suddenly realize what it was all about, Dad and the church, and what he was trying to do as a minister. His own job was on the line, and he was worried about Lou. That was the kind of person he was. I knew I could never be like that, not in a million years. I ran around his desk and gave him a big hug.

"Dad, it's not fair."

Dad returned my hug, then looked down with a smile as he brushed the hair back from my forehead. "God never promised that anything worthwhile would be fair or easy, Ruthie."

"I know, Dad, it's just that I want to help."

Dad gave me a squeeze and turned back to his desk. "You do help, Ruthie, just by being you. Now I have work here to finish up. I'll see you later."

As I walked home, I made up my mind. I *would* help Dad, whether he wanted me to or not. I hadn't had any luck with Kenny, but I was determined, somehow, in some way, to help Dad, even if it meant poking around St. Martin's against his orders. That was a promise.

·14·
THE RAFFLE TICKETS

THE ONLY THING I COULD THINK of right off to help Dad was to check the pile of yellow papers on the Choir Room piano to see if they were the anonymous letters or not. But I was too late. Though I ran down to the church first thing Saturday morning, the yellow papers were gone. Mrs. Moorehead and Miss Kunzinger must have realized I'd seen them and whisked them away.

On Sunday, I went to church alone. With the wedding only six days away, Mom wanted the day free to do errands, so she went to the early service. I was glad to see the church full, at least fuller than it had been lately. People had come to support Dad, that's what. Then, as I left my pew after the service, I realized everyone was standing around in little groups, buzzing and whispering. I heard snatches of talk about Lou Dargie, and those anonymous letters, too. But I didn't want to listen to gossip. I *wouldn't* listen to gossip. I hurried up the aisle and into the entryway, almost bumping into Police Chief Nussen who was talking to two men I didn't know. Though the two men wore business suits like everyone else, they looked like their business suits meant business.

"Who are those men talking to Chief Nussen?" I asked, after Dad had greeted me at the door with a kiss.

"Two Secret Service agents come to talk to me."

Secret Service!

I mulled it over on the way home. Maybe the Treasury Department had gotten one of those anonymous yellow letters and sent the Secret Service out to investigate. They might even have a search warrant. Or maybe they had come about Lou Dargie. For some reason, I thought of those neatly sealed cartons I'd seen in the back of Dad's Toyota and hoped the Secret Service hadn't seen them too. But what difference did it make whether the Secret Service saw them or not? Even if they opened the cartons, I was sure all they'd find would be offering envelopes or church school material or something equally unexciting.

I was still thinking about the Secret Service as I walked up our front porch steps. Without warning, my feet shot out from under me. I grabbed the railing just in time to keep from falling. The stairs were covered with slippery, wet oak leaves. Mom had asked me to sweep them off and I'd forgotten. I had better get at it. When I returned with a broom, I noticed an envelope sticking out of our mailbox. Had it been there when I'd gone into the house? I didn't think so, but I wasn't sure. I took it out of the box. There was no stamp on it, just a name. Ruth Saunders. My name!

Really curious now, I propped the broom against the front door and ripped open the envelope. A yellow paper was folded up inside. It was probably one of those anonymous letters like everyone else had gotten. I unfolded it and read.

DEAR RUTH,

The enclosed, I believe, is yours.

I'm sure you've been told not to interfere in places where you don't belong. Because you don't seem to pay much attention, I'll repeat it. Stay away from St. Martin's! PLEASE.

It was neatly typed, but not signed. My heart began to beat so hard, I wondered if I could really hear it, or whether that was just my imagination. I turned the envelope upside down and shook it. To my surprise, my book of Band raffle tickets fell out. Why, I'd lost them out of my slicker pocket weeks ago. They had, in fact, been missing since about that time Mr. Edmonds had found me in the church basement. I tried to think what I'd had on, that day. It had been raining, I remembered that, so I probably was wearing my slicker. The raffle tickets must have fallen out of my slicker pocket down in the church basement, and Mr. Edmonds had picked them up.

Mr. Edmonds had written this letter! That meant he had probably written the anonymous letter to all the church members as well. It had to be Mr. Edmonds. He and Dad were the only ones who knew I had been wandering around the church where I didn't belong. I remembered how relieved I had been that afternoon when I realized it was Mr. Edmonds who had followed me down those basement stairs and not Lou. That's how dumb I was. I pictured skinny, praying mantis Mr. Edmonds, and shuddered.

As I swept off the leaves, I tried to decide what to do.

Probably Dad should know about Mr. Edmonds's letter. But I had promised myself to help Dad, and I didn't see how showing him this letter would help. If Dad read it, he might think I had been hanging around the church again after he had told me not to. Besides, it would mean I'd have to explain how Mr. Edmonds had found me in the church basement. No, I decided, showing Dad this letter wouldn't help him one bit.

When I was done with sweeping, I ate the lunch Mom had left and started my homework. Still, Dad didn't come home. I couldn't imagine why he was so late. Right in the middle of an unsolvable math problem, I had the sudden, horrible thought that the Secret Service had arrested him. But they'd have to let him come home first, wouldn't they? I thought so, but I wasn't sure. Our old house had never seemed so empty. Or big. It creaked and groaned under the poking fingers of a cold November wind. I gave up on my homework and snuggled down with Tippy under an afghan and watched TV.

Finally, at four o'clock, Dad came home. He tried to act as if nothing had happened. He ate his dried-out tuna casserole lunch and read the Sunday paper, or at least pretended to read the Sunday paper. A couple of times I started to ask what the Secret Service had wanted, but Dad must have had his ESP tuned in. Every time I got up the courage to ask him, he maneuvered the conversation to something else.

As for the yellow letter I'd gotten, it was in my jeans' pocket along with the book of raffle tickets. Half a dozen times I pulled out the letter to show Dad, and just as many times shoved it back in. At last, while Dad was on the phone, I made up my mind. I'd let him read the letter and get his opinion. I took out the now dirty and wrinkled letter, reread it for about the tenth time, and flipped through the book of raffle tickets. Hey, wait a minute. I saw something I hadn't noticed before. My name and address were on every single receipt. I had forgotten that Phyllis had filled in all the stubs for me.

I heard Dad hang up the phone. Quickly I stuffed the letter and the raffle book back in my pocket and grabbed the Sunday funnies. Maybe Mr. Edmonds had found my tickets and maybe he hadn't. With my name and address on them like that, *anyone* could have found them in the church basement and known that they were mine.

·15·
REHEARSAL TIME

LATE THAT NIGHT, SUNDAY, Janice arrived home to spend the week getting ready for the wedding. It was wonderful to see her. But having her home changed everything. The wedding took over our whole lives. There were a million presents to open. The phone never stopped ringing, and neither did the doorbell. On both Monday and Tuesday nights, Mom, Janice, and I went to bridal showers, plus my brides-maid's dress needed two more fittings before Olga finally got it right. For now, school and worrying about Kenny were lost causes. At least all the running around gave me an excuse not to do anything about that letter I'd gotten. I stuck it in my sock drawer and tried to forget it.

In one way I was counting the days until Saturday and the wedding and couldn't wait. In another way, I hated to see the week pass. Dad had asked the bishop to give him until after the wedding to settle things at St. Martin's, and nothing was any more settled now than it had ever been. And despite all my big promises, I'd been no help at all.

Then, to complicate an already frantic week, St. Martin's Nearly New Shop had more trouble with counterfeit money. Luckily, this time one of the ladies was suspicious of a pile of tens in the cash register and pulled them out before any customers got stuck. Sure enough, the bank said the bills were counterfeit. The Secret Service descended on the Nearly New like locusts and questioned everyone, which really panicked all the ladies. I hoped they questioned Mrs. Moorehead, but good. I still remembered that day she'd switched those bills from her pocketbook into the cash register.

Then, just when I thought I'd never get it all together for the wedding, it was five o'clock Friday night and time for the wedding rehearsal. It had been drizzling all day, but at five o'clock on the dot, it started to pour. I checked the weather forecast for Saturday. Overcast with clouds was predicted, but no rain. Please, dear God, no rain.

All four ushers were late. They were driving straight to the church from New Haven, but by 5:20 they still hadn't showed up. At least Tom, his best man, and the bishop were all at the church on time. Smart Janice had come up with the idea of having Bishop Bayley perform the wedding, which left Dad free to escort her down the aisle like any other father of the bride. Janice was thoughtful, too. She asked Phyllis to assist the bishop at the altar, light the candles as acolyte, and come to the rehearsal dinner party afterward.

While we waited for the ushers, Nancy, one of Janice's friends from Yale, practiced her flute solo. I was no music critic, but I thought it sounded terrible.

In fact, the whole rehearsal was turning out to be a disaster. The church had never looked gloomier. All the overhead lantern lights were on, but they threw such an ugly glare, we all looked pasty white, with hollow pits for eyes. The rain drummed so hard on the slate roof above us, the damp seeped right through the cold stone walls. Phyllis and I were the only ones taking the rehearsal seriously. Everybody else was kidding around, and even Mom wasn't very excited when the ushers strolled in at 5:30. Maybe they'd all been in enough weddings to know what to do, but I was a wreck.

There I was, first down that long aisle, with Miss Kunzinger playing something that Tom and Janice had picked out that I didn't recognize. All my practicing with a tape of the Wedding March from the library didn't help one bit. I didn't know whether to glide, step-and-hesitate, or just plain walk. Tom, his best man, and the bishop standing at the chancel steps looked as far away as if I were seeing them through the wrong end of a telescope. To make matters worse, Phyllis, up by the altar, started giggling. I could have killed her.

But amazingly, between one practice and the next, everything went together. No one joked or kidded around, and I got down the aisle without tripping in my new high-heeled shoes. I even remembered to hold in my stomach. Phyllis didn't giggle, and the flute solo sounded better, and when I turned to watch Janice and Dad come down the aisle together, I saw that Dad had tears in his eyes. At that, I got pretty emotional myself, and I wondered how any of us would get through the real thing tomorrow.

Though we were all due back at Tom's house for

dinner after the rehearsal, no one seemed in a hurry to get started. Phyllis raced home to change her dress for the third time. Mom and Janice and Tom headed for the Seabury Room to check out the reception arrangements. The bridesmaids and ushers gathered at the back of the church talking and joking. Bishop Bayley and Dad disappeared in the direction of Dad's office, which left me alone with Miss Kunzinger.

Bang! Miss Kunzinger angrily slammed down the cover of her organ and stood up. "This organ hasn't sounded right since last summer. I'm sure those bellows weren't properly repaired. I'm going down to check them right now." She wasn't talking to me. I don't think she even realized I was there, as she picked up her key ring and started to leave.

"Mrs. Kunzinger, can I see you a minute?" It was Nancy, the flute soloist, running down the aisle. I smiled at the "Mrs.," which I knew annoyed Miss Kunzinger no end. "Can you help me with this middle section, Mrs. Kunzinger?" Nancy asked when she reached us.

Miss Kunzinger flipped back her long red hair. "It's Miss Kunzinger, and yes, I agree it needs work. We can go over it with the piano in the Choir Room." Miss Kunzinger led Nancy out the side sanctuary door, talking the whole time.

Miss Kunzinger had picked up her keys to unlock the Bellows Room door and check the bellows. I remembered the afternoon I had explored the basement, I'd found only one door locked, the door to the Bellows Room. At the time, I hadn't thought much about it, but now it occurred to me that there might be more reason to lock that door than just fear of vandalism.

I heard the bullets of rain pepper the church roof as I slowly, slowly moved my eyes in the direction of the organ. Miss Kunzinger had left her keys behind. They were right on top of the organ. This time it was as if I were looking through the right end of a telescope. The keys seemed to jump out at me.

I stared at the keys a good, long time. I was not, repeat, not to meddle in any church business. Those had been Dad's clear orders. On the other hand, I had promised myself I would help Dad, no matter what. And with Dad's deadline up tomorrow, it wasn't hard to guess what Dad and the bishop were discussing right now.

I picked up the key ring. If Miss Kunzinger had planned to check out the bellows, one of the keys on her key ring was sure to open that Bellows Room door. I didn't dare let myself think what I might find, let alone consider that what I was doing might be dangerous.

My first problem was to get into the basement without anyone seeing me. I couldn't go down the Seabury Room basement stairs. Mom was in there. She was busy, but she was never too busy not to ask questions. No, I'd have to go down those back basement stairs that Lou had used the day I'd seen him unloading packages from the Coles' Mercedes.

As I passed the Altar Guild room where the flowers were arranged and the altar hangings stored, I glanced in, not expecting to see anyone. But Mrs. Moorehead was there, dressed in a yellow Altar Guild smock, working at the sink with her back to the door. I couldn't resist making a face as I tiptoed past. Then I remembered that Mrs. Moorehead was on Altar Guild duty this month and was probably setting up for our family communion service tomorrow morning. That made me feel a little guilty, but not very.

A narrow back hall beyond the Altar Guild room led to a closed door. That, in turn, opened onto another little hall with a second door at the end of it. No wonder I'd never seen the back stairway before. Dad ʰad said the church had been added onto from every direction over the years, and I believed it. I opened the second door and, there, in front of me, was the rear entrance Lou had used the day I'd seen him from the school bus. A flight of stairs led down into the basement.

I closed the stairway door behind me and turned on the lights. I stood at the top, looking down. The stairs were steep and narrow, and I was wearing stockings, high-heeled shoes, and a new, full-skirted print dress. Maybe I should come back when I wasn't all dressed up. But that was no good. I had to do it now, before I changed my mind.

·16·
OFF KEY

WHEN I REACHED THE BOTTOM of the stairs, I looked back up, half-expecting to see the outside door burst open and someone charge down after me. But there was nothing to see but gray night shadows and nothing to hear but the patter of rain and the swish of moving traffic on the wet streets outside.

I searched along the cinder-block wall until I found a light switch. Click. The bare light bulb lit up the high-vaulted ceiling like some kind of ancient cobwebby catacomb. A trickle of water ran down the wall by the staircase where the rain leaked in. I was in the oldest part of the church.

Since I had to start somewhere, I turned left, and found myself in a long hallway. The light was dim, but I didn't see another switch. Slosh. I splashed right through a puddle in my new shoes. The water must seep right up through the floor here. I shivered, and my skin crawled with the thought of damp-basement creatures and moldy-green growth on the walls.

It wasn't until I reached the next corner that I saw something familiar on the wall, a faded poster for a rock mass that I remembered from last time I was down here. Now I knew where I was. The main part of the basement was left again, then straight ahead. That meant the Bellows Room must be around the next turn.

It was. I studied the words "Bellows Room" painted on the closed door. I gripped Miss Kunzinger's key ring so tightly, it hurt my hand. I couldn't hesitate. Miss Kunzinger might start looking for her keys. Or, someone might have seen me come down here, someone waiting to pounce. Don't clutch, I told myself. No one saw you, not one single person. Take a deep breath and get on with it.

I studied the lock. It was brand new. I held the sweaty key ring up to the light and picked out the newest looking key on it. But when I put it in the lock, it was much too big to fit. That meant I'd have to try every key on the ring. As I started to work my way around the key ring, I felt wet circles of sweat under my arms. I'd ruined my shoes and now I was ruining my dress. Worse than that, something was wrong. Not one key on Miss Kunzinger's ring fit the lock. But that didn't make sense. If Miss Kunzinger was coming down here to check the bellows, she'd certainly have the key.

I was right back where I started from. Only, if Dad ever knew what I was doing, he'd serve me my head on a platter, bridesmaid's hat and all. Scarier than that would be for someone else to find me, the someone who had returned my raffle tickets with that unsigned letter.

That possibility finished me. Anonymous letters,

locked doors, keys that should fit but didn't, were all too much to figure out. People, that's what I needed right now, and the sooner the better. I took off down the hall, half-slid at the turn by the poster, splattered through the puddle, and skidded around another corner, stopping short at the foot of the rear staircase. I'd never make it up those steep steps in high-heeled shoes. I kicked them off, picked up a shoe in either hand, and dashed up the stairs, two at a time, not breathing until I was safely at the top.

·17·
THE WEDDING

WHEN I WOKE UP SATURDAY MORNING, I lay in bed a long time with my eyes closed, just thinking. I hadn't told anyone at the party last night what had happened, or rather what hadn't happened, with Miss Kunzinger's keys and the Bellows Room lock. And no one had guessed what I'd been up to. Mom figured I'd gotten my shoes wet running from the church to the car through the rain, and I didn't set her straight. Thoughts of last night's downpour brought me up short. This was Janice's wedding day. How could I have forgotten? I rolled out of bed and raced to the window. The sky was gray. But over there, high up, I saw patches of blue through the oak trees' bony bare branches, which looked hopeful.

I remembered making my bed and dressing, but the rest of the day passed in a numb haze. The morning communion service, the brunch, getting into my Damson Plum dress, having Tom's sister make up my eyes, helping Janice button her gown, driving to the church, waiting for the music to begin.

Janice was beautiful. Dad had never looked handsomer. The bridesmaids and ushers were an autumnal tapestry of color, just the way Olga's Bridal Shoppe had promised. Even the church glowed, at least glowed as much as St. Martin's could ever glow. Tall candles at the end of each pew softened the overhead glare, and someone had had the good sense to turn up the heat. Flowers and gauzy green ferns around the altar hid the bleak stonework and dulled the hollow echoes of footsteps on the marble floor.

When the wedding music began and I started down the aisle, I was so carried away by the moment, I forgot to be nervous. Then I saw Mom in the first pew look back at me and smile encouragement through her tears. I missed a step, caught my heel in the hem of my dress, and almost tripped as I realized everyone else was staring back at me too. A blush started at my neck and flooded my face. In desperation, I focused my eyes on Tom, his best man, and the bishop standing at the chancel steps. Even halfway down the aisle, I could see a beady mustache of perspiration across Tom's upper lip. I felt better instantly. Tom was at least as nervous as I was, and Phyllis in her red acolyte robe up by the altar, looked even more nervous.

As soon as I was safely down the aisle, I relaxed. Now I could enjoy the wedding. But I relaxed too soon. Right in the middle of the flute solo, a familiar brown-white face peered around the end of the choir stalls up in the sanctuary. Tippy! His mouth was open in what looked like a grin, and his pink tongue hung out at a crazy angle. I heard Mom gasp with shock behind me. Ron Silver, our neighbor, was supposed to be at our house sitting for Tippy and the wedding presents. Tippy must have gotten out and followed us here. His eyesight was bad, but if he spotted any of us Saunders, he'd come running.

Luckily Phyllis was on the alert. She dropped out of sight behind the choir stalls. A moment later, her hand shot out and grabbed Tippy by the collar. Tippy let out with one quick yelp, but with the flute tootling away, nobody noticed. I hoped. Then all was quiet. Phyllis must have carried Tippy out the side sanctuary door. The flute solo had just ended when Phyllis finally reappeared. Without Tippy. I hadn't realized I was holding my breath until all the air went out of my lungs in a big sigh. Whew, if I was relieved, I could imagine how Mom felt.

Phyllis was the first one through the receiving line after the wedding. "Did you hear Tippy bark? I thought I'd die. I shut him up in your father's office." Phyllis grinned. "Now on to the punch."

I watched Phyllis teeter over to the punch bowl in her new high heels. Mom and Dad had planned to serve wine punch, then decided on plain fruit punch at the last minute, but I'd forgotten to tell Phyllis about the switch. She filled her cup, raised it to me in a toast, then started drinking. I was grinning myself. The wedding was over, and Tippy hadn't spoiled it. Janice was married, and I hadn't fallen on my face.

I had dreaded the receiving line, but it turned out to be easy. In fact, I enjoyed it. I had been paying so much attention to the few troublemakers at the church, I'd forgotten about all the people who loved St. Martin's and really cared about us Saunders. Besides, I didn't have to think of anything to say to them. They had to think of something to say to me, and since most of them told me I looked pretty, all I had to come up with was "thank you." Even without pierced ears they were calling me pretty. Maybe it was the eye makeup and the bridesmaid's hat that fooled them.

The last guests had just finished going through the receiving line when I saw a latecomer pause at the door and look around. It was Lou Dargie, all dressed up in a tan suit with a tan and red tie, looking paler than ever. Lou Dargie! For hours I hadn't given one thought to counterfeiting, Secret Service, Dad's deadline or anything in the world but the wedding. I hadn't even thought of Kenny all day. Now seeing Lou Dargie, everything rushed over me like a wave crashing.

I hurried over to Dad, who was talking with Mr. and Mrs. Cole and two people I didn't know, and grabbed his sleeve and pulled him aside. "Dad, Lou is here."

Dad put his arm around my shoulders and smiled at me. "I know, isn't it wonderful? I persuaded the warden to let Lou come to the wedding. Not only that, but he starts working again for us next week on a trial basis."

"Lou's coming back to St. Martin's?" Mrs. Cole had edged up behind Dad. She must have been eavesdropping. I should know. It took one to spot one. Mr. Cole strolled over, too, trying to act casual.

"Yes, it's a wedding present from me to Lou," Dad said. "Now if you'll excuse me, I'd like to make him feel welcome."

Speechless, I watched Dad head in Lou's direction. I couldn't believe it. Lou showing up had spoiled my day. No, today was Janice's wedding day, and I wouldn't let Lou spoil it, no matter what. Besides, he was here, and there was nothing I could do about it. I'd just forget Lou and get something to eat, that's what. Besides, I was famished. I hadn't had any breakfast, and I'd hardly eaten a bite at the brunch. But there were only a couple of sandwiches left, and the punch bowl was empty. I ate the last two sandwiches, then carried the empty platters out to the kitchen.

"We're out of sandwiches and punch, Mrs. Trent," I said. Mrs. Trent was a member of St. Martin's who catered parties and weddings.

"Excuse me, Ruth."

I jumped out of the way. Mr. Edmonds was right behind me, holding the empty punch bowl. He set it on the counter. "I'm afraid this needs a refill, Mrs. Trent," he said.

Mrs. Trent seemed flustered. "I didn't realize the food would run out so quickly. I'd better get the other punch bowl. Can I borrow your keys to open the pantry closet, Mr. Edmonds?"

"Let me get it for you." Mr. Edmonds pulled out his key ring and stepped into the pantry, reappearing in a minute with the punch bowl.

By the time Mrs. Trent filled both punch bowls, I had arranged more sandwiches on the platters. Mr. Edmonds picked up one of the punch bowls, and carried it back into the Seabury Room, followed by me with the sandwiches. Phyllis was waiting with her empty cup.

"This punch is great." She poured herself more. Her words sounded slurred, and she was swaying. I didn't know whether that was from her high heels or whether she thought she was getting drunk.

"I saw your dog show up at the wedding," a voice behind me announced.

I didn't even have to turn around to know who it was. Sure enough, Oliver Cole stood at the table stuffing nuts into his mouth with both hands. Count on Oliver to have spotted Tippy.

"Tippy's a member of our family. He had every right to be there."

"If he's such a great member of your family, where is he now?"

Oh, no, I'd forgotten Tippy. He wasn't here because he was still in Dad's office where Phyllis had put him. And Tippy hated to be shut up anywhere. I'd better phone Ron Silver right away to come and get him.

When I opened the office door, Tippy leapt on me with hysterical barking. I pushed him down, afraid of paw prints on my beautiful dress. Then, to make up for hurting his feelings, I hugged him, still careful not to muss my dress. For once he smelled great. Phyllis and I had given him a bath yesterday with a special flea-killing, itch-proof soap. "I'm glad you came to the wedding, Tip," I whispered.

After I'd phoned Ron to tell him I'd wait with Tippy in Dad's office, I sat down at Dad's desk. To pass the time, I idly doodled hearts and wedding rings on a scratch pad. I doodled Janice's and Tom's initials, then without thinking, I doodled mine and Kenny's. R. B. S. and K.L.H. L. for Louis. I'd seen it on Kenny's class schedule. Kenny. I should face Kenny and have it out with him, not just stammer around like I had last time. If Dad's being a minister was what really bugged him, then he had to tell me. But it was easier said than done. I'd blown it once. I'd never get up the courage again . . .

I was thinking about Kenny, but I was doodling a row of barred prison windows. I stared at the paper.

Whatever made me do that? Because something reminded me of Lou, that's what. I put down my pencil and studied Dad's desk. No wonder I was reminded of Lou. Two sets of keys lay right in front of me on the blotter, one was Dad's, labeled "Rector," and the other was Lou's, labeled "Sexton." Dad must have gotten out the sexton key ring to give back to Lou.

I picked up both sets of keys and walked over to the window. Pulling aside the curtain, I looked out. The day had completely cleared. It was cold and windy, with high, white clouds and a bright sun that reminded me of northern California at its best.

I glanced across the courtyard into the Seabury Room directly opposite. The Seabury Room windows were leaded diamond panes that blurred everything. I saw people moving back and forth indistinctly and a long flash of white that must have been Janice.

It had been a perfect wedding. Almost perfect, anyway. If only I could solve Dad's problems as a wedding present from me to him, just like he'd done for Lou. I squeezed the key rings tight in my hands as I willed myself to think of something ... anything. ... The keys cut into my palms. I opened them and stared at the two key rings. Keys ... keys ... everyone had keys. Dad's "Rector" keys, Lou's "Sexton" keys, Mrs. Cole's "Secretary" keys, Mr. Edmonds's "Grounds" keys, Mrs. Moorehead's "Women's Guild" keys, Miss Kunzinger's "Organist" keys. Six sets of keys and six people who could get into any room at St. Martin's.

An idea was slowly coming to me, sprouting, growing, sending out roots. Maybe, just maybe, I could help Dad. But I'd have to do it now, during the reception. I'd never have the same chance again. Tippy limped over to the window and stood beside me. I leaned down and rubbed the soft fur of his throat.

"Tippy, as soon as Ron comes to pick you up, I'm going to give it a try." Saying the words out loud made it a commitment. Now I'd have to go through with it.

·18·
BEHIND
THE BOUQUET

AFTER RON SILVER LEFT WITH TIPPY, I headed back to the Seabury Room. I had both Lou's "Sexton" keys and Dad's "Rector" keys with me. That was the easy part. Now came the hard.

The reception was in full swing. I couldn't believe my eyes. Stiff, uptight Miss Kunzinger was pounding away on the piano, and she was good. Janice had taken off her veil, and she and Tom and most of the guests had gathered around the piano and were singing along. Everyone having a good time was fine with me. No one would notice what I was up to.

My bridesmaid's bouquet was still on the window-sill where I'd left it. I slipped the two sets of keys behind it, then put my hat on the sill, too. Much as I loved it, the floppy brim got in my way. I looked all over the room for Mrs. Cole, but I didn't see her anywhere, or Mr. Cole either, though Oliver and Lisa certainly hadn't left yet. Lisa was running back and forth over by the windows with a friend, acting crazy.

Oliver was still gorging himself at the food table, as if he hadn't eaten for a week. Even his eyeglasses were smeared with food.

"Where's your mother, Oliver?" I asked.

Oliver stuffed a whole mushroom sandwich in his mouth before answering. "Mom and Dad are out in the hall having a big fight."

What did he mean? No one had a fight at a wedding reception. I went out into the hall and found that Oliver, as usual, was right. I heard the Coles before I saw them.

"You promised you'd quit after the wedding and that means today," Mr. Cole was practically shouting.

"I'm not going to quit and you know it," Mrs. Cole snapped back.

"We have more than enough money now to manage . . ."

I had no time to spare for eavesdropping. I arranged my face in a smile and walked around the corner looking my most innocent. "Hi, Mrs. Cole, Oliver told me you were out here."

Mr. and Mrs. Cole were facing each other off, like Tippy and Ron Silver's cat. "What is it, Ruth?" Mr. Cole demanded.

I ran my tongue around my lips to unglue my Barbie-doll smile. "Dad wants me to get something from his office, and he doesn't have his keys. Can I borrow yours, Mrs. Cole?" It wasn't a complete lie. Dad didn't have his keys. I did. Still, I was sure my red face would give me away.

But Mrs. Cole wasn't noticing anything. Her eyes were blinking a mile a minute, and her hands were practically shaking as she opened her pocketbook, yanked out her key ring and slapped it in my hand. "Here. That man would forget his keys if they were hanging around his neck."

Any other time I would have burned at the insult, but now I didn't care. Mrs. Cole probably wouldn't have handed over her keys if she hadn't been in such a bad mood. I hid Mrs. Cole's "Secretary" keys behind my bouquet with the others, then looked for Mr. Edmonds.

There he was, across the room, the tallest man in a crowd of people buzzing around the bishop, like bees around clover. As I edged into the group, everyone made way for me, oh-ing and ah-ing about how cute I was. Privilege, that's what being a bridesmaid meant.

"Here's our little maid of honor," the bishop announced, and I saw no reason to correct him. After all, walking down the aisle first was almost as important as being maid of honor, and a lot harder.

Still, right now wasn't the best moment to be the center of attention. I felt myself blush. "Ah ... Mr. Edmonds, ah, can I borrow your church keys, please? Dad asked me to get something out of his office and he doesn't have his." I said the words so fast, Mr. Edmonds must have guessed I'd rehearsed it.

But Mr. Edmonds didn't notice any more than Mrs. Cole had. He opened his hands, as if to show me they were empty. "I'd be happy to, Ruth, but I left them home."

"But you used them to get the punch bowl from the pantry, remember?"

Now it was Mr. Edmonds's turn to look embarrassed. He cleared his throat as he glanced at the bishop, then back at me. "Of course, I forgot," he apologized, as he pulled his keys from his pocket and gave them to me.

Mr. Edmonds's "Grounds" keys went behind my bouquet with the others. Now for Miss Kunzinger. Even though I had tried her keys last night, I wanted to be perfectly sure. She was still playing the piano. Her head was back, and her long, red hair was swinging in rhythm to the music. With everyone gathered around the piano like that, there was no way I could ask Miss Kunzinger for her keys without being asked a lot of questions in return. Then I remembered. Miss Kunzinger never carried a pocketbook. I just bet her keys were on the piano in the Choir Room where she usually left them. I'd pick them up later. That left only Mrs. Moorehead.

I looked over the big room. Almost everyone was around the piano. Even Mr. Edmonds and Bishop Bayley had wandered over. Mom and Mrs. Mitchell, Tom's mother, stood together singing, Mom in her Golden Maize Mother of the Bride dress, and Mrs. Mitchell in Sage Green. They seemed to be enjoying themselves. Dad and Lou were on the edge of the group, with Dad trying to encourage Lou to join in. The ushers, bridesmaids, and guests were all there, everyone but Mrs. Moorehead. She must have gone home.

Gross. I needed all six sets of keys for my plan to work. Well, it couldn't be helped. I'd have to make do with what I had. And right now, with everyone's attention on Miss Kunzinger was a good time to slip out.

I picked up my bouquet and all the keys with it. Luckily, it was a trailing arrangement of chrysanthemums and ivy that was perfect camouflage for the keys. I turned to leave, then hesitated. Someone, somehow, should know where I was going.

Phyllis had drifted over to the food table to refill her punch cup. Oliver stood at the far end of the table, resting his chin in his hands, as if gathering strength to tackle the food again.

"Sst, Phyllis," I hissed to get her attention. When she turned around, I noticed black mascara smudges under her eyes, and I wondered if my eye makeup was smeared too.

"Listen, Phyllis." I looked straight at her and spoke distinctly. "I'm going down to the basement on an errand. If I'm not back in fifteen minutes, tell Dad to come down to the Bellows Room and find me. Did you get that? The Bellows Room in fifteen minutes."

"What do you mean? What are you going to do in the Bellows Room?"

"I'll tell you later, I promise. Right now repeat the message so I know you have it straight."

"Don't worry. I got it. If you're not back in fifteen minutes, tell your father to come get you in the Bellows Room."

She was talking too loud, and her words ran together, but she had the message right. Phyllis was too sharp not to get it right. Besides, she only imagined she was high. I'd seen Mrs. Trent make that punch out of straight fruit juice and soda water.

As I hurried through the kitchen with my bouquet and keys, I noticed Mrs. Trent was frantically making more sandwiches. She'd really lucked out having Oliver Cole show up.

When I stepped out the back kitchen door, the

corridor was empty. The music and singing from the Seabury Room, though fainter, still sounded gay, I hoped it stayed that way and kept everyone happy so that no one missed me. Holding up my unfamiliar long skirts, I jogged down the hall toward the Choir Room. Miss Kunzinger's keys were right on the piano where I had guessed they would be. It was a good luck sign, I just knew it, like rolling doubles on the first backgammon throw.

I had to go through the church itself. It was the only way I knew to get to those back basement stairs. I pulled open the church door and stepped inside. It was hard to believe there had been a wedding here only an hour or so ago. The church had been golden and warm and perfumy. Now it was empty and cold. The smell of wax still hung in the air, but now the burnt-down candles looked droopy and sad. The huge stone pillars loomed like giant sentinels as the November dusk threw long shadows into the dark corners. Only the altar was lit. I glanced at it, then stopped short. Instead of two vases of flowers on the altar, there was only one. As soon as I saw that, I knew where Mrs. Moorehead was. She hadn't gone home. She was on Altar Guild duty this month and was straightening up after the wedding. She must have taken the flowers out to the Altar Guild room.

I was right. She was coming out of the Altar Guild room just as I rushed around the corner. We almost collided. I think if her black hair hadn't been so stuck together with spray, it would have stood on end. She clutched her chest dramatically.

"Ruth, you frightened me!"

"I'm sorry, Mrs. Moorehead. I just wanted to borrow

your keys to get something for Dad from his office. He doesn't have his." I pointed to her "Women's Guild" key ring on the counter and clenched my own fistful of keys tight in my other hand to keep them from rattling.

"I . . . I don't think so. No, I'm afraid not."

I couldn't hesitate now, not when I had thought Mrs. Moorehead was gone and I had found her. I surprised even myself by marching right over to the counter and picking up her keys. "I'll bring them back in ten minutes, I promise."

My nerve must have surprised Mrs. Moorehead as much as it did me. She just stared as I thanked her and walked out. I headed back into the church as if I were returning to the reception. Then I scurried behind one of the dark side pews and crouched out of sight. Pretty soon I heard the tap of Mrs. Moorehead's heels click up the marble altar steps as she returned for the second vase of flowers. The minute her back was turned, I ducked out the side door, ran on tiptoe past the empty Altar Guild room, and down the hall to the door at the end of it. I closed it quietly behind me, scooted the short distance to the second door and closed that quietly behind me, too.

My plan had worked perfectly. "I had six sets of keys, every one I wanted. No one had seen me and I would be back before I was missed. So then why was my heart pounding ready to burst through my padded bra as I tucked my Damson Plum skirt tight around me and started down the narrow basement stairs?

·19·
KEY TO
THE LOCK

BY THE TIME I REACHED THE BELLOWS ROOM, I was panting like Tippy after a hard run. I leaned my head against the door and closed my eyes. It was terribly quiet. After the singing and laughter and confusion of the reception, the basement was like a giant damp tomb. I was too far away even to hear the friendly rumble of the furnace. I was alone, completely alone. Or, maybe I wasn't. My eyes flew open as I checked the hall in both directions. Of course I was alone. What did I expect?

I looked at the lock. Though it was shiny-brass new, I was sure it wasn't the same lock that the church had installed last summer after the bellows were slit. If it were, one of Miss Kunzinger's keys should have opened it. But, unless I'd made a mistake yesterday, none of her keys fit. Someone had changed the lock, and that someone must have the key to open it. I didn't know which ring that key would be on, but all six rings were neatly labeled. I was sure it wouldn't be one of Dad's keys, but trying his set would give me the perfect proof that he was innocent.

I laid my bouquet on the floor beside the door and piled all the key rings beside it. Now that I was actually starting, I felt better. I didn't dare rush it, but I couldn't waste time either.

I picked up the first key ring from the floor and, starting with the key nearest to the label, tried every key on it. Not one of them fit the lock. I laid that set of keys on the floor, separate from the rest, and picked up a second set. None of those keys fit the lock either. I dropped the second key ring in the discard pile and tried the third, and then the fourth. With no luck. By the time I started on the fifth key ring, the filmy cape of my dress clung damply to my back. All the water in me must be coming out in perspiration. My mouth was so dry, I had to work up spit to swallow.

I had made my way almost completely around the fifth set of keys when I heard a soft whistle. The sound startled me, until I realized it was me, sucking in my breath. The next to last key had slipped right into the lock without pushing or poking, or any effort at all. The lock clicked as I turned it. Made for each other. I pulled the key out of the door and reread the label. Incredible!

I reached out to open the door, then jerked my hand back. Bats, creatures, winged horrors might fly out at me. A corpse. A booby trap set to go off if anyone crossed the threshold. I took a step backwards. All I had to do was pick up my bouquet and keys, go back to the reception, and let someone else take over.

Dad wouldn't do that. He always plowed ahead, even if it meant trouble. Besides, I was the one who had gotten this far on my own. I had to find out what was inside. I turned the knob and pushed the door open.

The glare of the hall light bulb lit up the room well enough to see. It was smaller than I had expected and was completely filled with what must be the bellows, great leather lungs set in a wooden frame attached to pipes and pumps that probably led to the organ upstairs. That was it. Before my heart was ready to burst out of my chest. Now it didn't seem to be beating. All that was in the Bellows Room was bellows.

I couldn't believe I had been so wrong. I was positive I'd find something in here that would solve all Dad's problems. I'd even been afraid to come in this dumb room, and all that was in here were stupid bellows.

I was just about to slam the door in total fury and frustration, when I noticed another door beyond the bellows, a swinging door with "Storage" painted on it. It was probably just another closet like all the rest of the closets in this basement, full of junk. Still, I might as well check it out.

The storage-room door swung open easily. But it was too dark to see inside. I ran my hand along the rough plaster wall until I found a switch. I pressed it, and an overhead fluorescent light flickered on in spurts. I paused, my hand still on the light switch and stared. This wasn't a closet crammed with junk at all. It was a little room, neatly organized from top to bottom. A big piece of machinery ran along one wall. I'd never seen a printing press before, but I was sure that's what I was looking at. It was sky blue, about four feet high and five or six feet long, with canvas conveyor tapes leading into three rollers at one end. Sheets of white paper were stacked in front of the rollers, with a tray at the opposite end to catch what came out. A big papercutter on a table was surrounded by orderly piles of metal boxes. And, under the table were the rolls of paper wrapped in plastic that I'd first seen in the Coles' basement. That was what Lou had been delivering after all!

This was it. I'd done it. I'd found the counterfeiting setup. But instead of feeling thrilled out of my mind the way I thought I would, I felt only numb. Stiff as a mechanical doll, I laid the key ring on the table and picked up one of the metal boxes. It was the size of a shoe box, and heavy. Slowly, I unfastened the latch and opened the cover. It was filled with packages of carefully wrapped ten dollar bills. I'd heard about the wind being knocked right out of a person, and that was what happened to me. Luckily, there was a chair by the table. I sank down on it, completely breathless.

There had to be hundreds and hundreds of dollars in the box, and the table was piled with boxes. I opened a second box. It was full of tens just like the first. I had never seen so much money in my life and every bit of it must be counterfeit. All the proof was here. And I had the labeled key that fit the new Bellows Room lock.

A scraping noise behind me, like a foot moving across concrete, sent the little hairs along my arms on end. I spun around. Someone was standing in the Bellows Room doorway. Under the white glare of the fluorescent light, I was as visible as a Christmas tree, but the person in the doorway was completely hidden by the shadows. Too terrified to make a sound, I just sat there, gripping my chair with both hands.

"Ruth, are you all right? Your friend Phyllis sent me down here to find you. What on earth are you doing?"

"Mr. Edmonds." My voice was a squeak. All I could think was that Phyllis had fouled me up. She was to have told Dad to come down for me.

It was as if Mr. Edmonds knew what I was thinking. "Phyllis didn't want to bother your father, so she asked me to check on you instead." Mr. Edmonds ducked under the low door frame and walked past the bellows to stand in the storage-room doorway. The bright light deepened the lines in his thin Abraham Lincoln face. Craggy was the best word to describe Mr. Edmonds.

"What is all this equipment, and what are you doing down here, Ruth?" He gave me a puzzled smile.

I shook my head, unable to answer. I was on my feet without knowing how I got out of my chair.

"You'd better come with me. They'll be looking for you, and Janice is about to cut the cake." Mr. Edmonds spoke slowly, as if I were simpleminded.

I felt simpleminded. How could everyone upstairs be singing and eating and cutting cakes, while I was down here having this unreal conversation?

Mr. Edmonds smiled patiently and reached out as if to take my arm. I jumped back, hitting the table so hard a pile of gray boxes crashed to the floor.

"No!" I cried.

Mr. Edmonds's smile was gone instantly, and just as instantly, I realized my mistake. He had been feeling me out, trying to decide how much I knew. My panic told him everything, that I had gotten into the room with *his* key, that I knew the printing press was *his* printing press, that the counterfeit money was *his* money. And those boxes! I should have realized right away that they were burial urns. No wonder Mr. Edmonds didn't want anyone else working around the columbarium. He was storing counterfeit money in the empty urns.

"Help, somebody! Help!"

In two steps Mr. Edmonds was across the room. I

didn't wait to find out what he planned to do. I just snatched a metal box from the table and heaved it at him. It only caught him on the shoulder, but he fell back with a grunt of surprise. The box clattered to the floor, smashing open, and scattering packages of bills.

In that second of confusion, I raced through the Bellows Room and out the door, slamming it shut behind me. Without thinking, I started up the hall in the direction from which I had come. Dumb! The other way led through the main basement and right up into the Seabury Room. But it was too late to change direction now. I heard the Bellows Room door bang open and Mr. Edmonds's heavy footsteps thud after me. I wanted to scream, howl, cry for help, but I had no breath to do anything but run.

Then, without warning, my feet flew out from under me and I was falling. I had slipped in the forgotten puddle. I flailed my arms like a windmill trying to regain my balance, but it was no good. My legs tangled up in my long skirts, and I landed on my tailbone with a burst of pain. I struggled to get up, but Mr. Edmonds was right beside me. He scooped me up and set me on my feet.

"Help!" It was the last word I got out. Mr. Edmonds's big hand stifled my scream. I couldn't breathe. I shook my head back and forth, frantically digging at his hand with my nails to free my nose.

Mr. Edmonds wrenched my arm up behind my back and shoved me forward. I felt my dress rip under my arm, and for some reason that made me angrier than anything. Furious, I tried to bite his hand, but he held my jaws so tight I couldn't open my mouth. All of a sudden, he yanked me to a stop.

"My keys. I have to go back for them."

Of course. His key ring labeled "Grounds" was back on the storage-room table with all the counterfeit money. Anyone finding his keys would figure it out like I had.

Mr. Edmonds jerked me around and started me back in the direction of the Bellows Room. We splashed through the puddle without trying to go around it. His grip on me was iron. How could anyone so thin be so strong?

When we reached the Bellows Room, Mr. Edmonds shoved me past the bellows into the storage room. He had already pocketed his keys, when I heard a faraway voice calling.

"Ruthie. Ruthie, Baby, are you down here?"

The shout came from such an echoey distance, it could have been God. It was just as good as God. It was Dad. Phyllis had sent him down for me after all.

"Hhheellmm." Though I shouted all sorts of things, like "help" and "here I am," and "come get me," the huge hand over my mouth smothered my cries.

But Dad's shout must have undone Mr. Edmonds. He couldn't seem to decide what to do. One moment he pushed me toward the Bellows Room door, and the next he pulled me back. Then his hold on me tightened, as if he had made up his mind. He clamped his hand over my nose, cutting off my air. I struggled and kicked. I heard Dad call my name again, but this time he seemed farther away. The light dimmed, too. I was drifting off like the time I'd had gas at the dentist.

"What happened?" It was Dad's voice. Somehow I had the sense of him bending over me. I seemed to be propped up in a chair.

"Phyllis asked. ..." That was Mr. Edmonds. "... Ruth unconscious on the floor ... a man hiding

. . . hit me . . . see to Ruth. I'll go after him."

Though the words faded in and out, I understood enough to know something was wrong. I tried to shake my head "no," but I didn't have the strength. I heard footsteps running, familiar heavy footsteps. They were Mr. Edmonds's footsteps running . . . running away. . . .

I wondered if it was the eye makeup that made my eyelids so heavy. And the white light was painful, as Dad's worried face gradually came into focus. There was Lou, too, peering over Dad's shoulder.

"Baby, are you all right?" Dad asked.

I took a sweet, lung-filling breath. "No one was hiding . . . it was Mr. Edmonds. . . ."

"Wally Edmonds? Wally ran after the man who hurt you."

"Mr. Edmonds hurt me." It was hard to talk. My mouth was sore, so were my nose and jaw. Even my teeth ached.

Lou understood right away. "It's Edmonds you want, Mr. Saunders. Let me go after him."

Dad dismissed Lou with a wave of his hand as if he didn't care. His eyes were still anxiously searching my face. Again, I heard footsteps running. This time they were Lou's.

"All this machinery, the money on the floor. You found the counterfeiters, didn't you, Ruthie?"

I nodded, but it still hurt too much to talk.

"You did this for me, took the risk. . . ."

I nodded again.

"It was wrong, you know that, Ruthie. Anything could have happened . . . it almost did. . . " Dad's voice was hoarse.

Warm tears clouded my eyes.

"This is no time to talk. All I want right now is to get

you out of here before anything else happens." Dad reached down and helped me up from the chair. Then, supporting most of my weight, he guided me toward the Bellows Room door. I had to be hallucinating. Oliver Cole stood in the doorway. Oliver Cole!

Dad seemed surprised too. "Oliver, I forgot about you. Are you okay?"

Oliver stepped aside to let us pass. "Sure. I showed Lou which way Mr. Edmonds went."

Oliver was one complication too many to figure out. "Why is Oliver here?"

"Oliver gave me your message," Dad answered.

"No, Phyllis was supposed to give you the message."

"Phyllis didn't have anything to do with it. Oliver brought me down here himself."

Oliver must have been eavesdropping on the directions I'd given Phyllis. Oliver's snooping had saved me. I looked at his punch-streaked face and dark eyes, magnified by his thick glasses. His pre-tied bow tie hung off one collar, and his shirttails were out. I had to smile. Oliver and I were two of a kind, that's what.

Still holding onto Dad with one arm, I hugged Oliver with the other. "Thanks for keeping your eye on me, Ol."

But Oliver squirmed away and took off down the hall toward the main basement room with Dad and me following slowly behind.

·20·
THE SKIERS

THIS TIME KENNY COULDN'T AVOID ME. I got right behind him in the chair-lift line, and that wasn't easy. It was my first ski trip and getting around on skis was a lot harder than I had thought it would be. But I managed. Kenny looked really surprised when I got on the chair with him and we started up the lift together.

I had planned for days what I would say, but now nothing came to me but a "Hi, Kenny."

Kenny wasn't much more original. "Hi," he said, swallowing so hard his Adam's apple went almost up to his chin, then back down again. "I read about you in the newspaper," he mumbled, without looking at me. He must have figured since he couldn't escape me this time by ducking into the boys' room, he'd try to make the best of it.

"You mean the article about the wedding?"

"No, about that man you caught with the counterfeit stuff."

The wind rocked our chair. It wasn't a long ride and it wasn't very steep, but I held on tight to the safety bar. Nothing about skiing had turned out to be easy. "Lou Dargie helped catch Mr. Edmonds, too," I said.

"Who?" Kenny still hadn't looked at me.

"Lou is our church sexton. He caught Mr. Edmonds the night of the wedding in the church parking lot and decked him. At first I thought Lou was in the counterfeiting business with the Coles, but Lou and the Coles didn't have anything to do with it. See, Mr. Edmonds had someone from his plant order the special one hundred percent rag paper from Mr. Cole that I saw Lou deliver to the church." Before I couldn't think of anything to say, and now I was saying too much.

Kenny not only looked embarrassed, but now he looked confused as well.

I tried to explain. "Mr. Edmonds was afraid Lou would find his printing press in the Bellows Room, so when he heard Lou on the phone making bets, he turned Lou in to the warden at the prison." Mr. Edmonds had tried to scare me off, too, with that letter and the raffle tickets he'd stuck in my mailbox. And he'd done pretty well.

"Mom and I drove past Edmonds's house. If he could live in such a huge house with a pool and a tennis court, how come he had to make counterfeit money?" Kenny was beginning to sound interested.

"Mr. Edmonds's company went bankrupt, so he owed a lot of money, thousands and thousands, I guess. He turned out counterfeit money to tide him over, is what Dad said."

The steady whine of the chair lift motor was reassuring, but I didn't like the way the chairs bumped over the rollers as we passed each tower. I tightened my grip on the safety bar as a gust of wind rocked our chair. I noticed that Kenny was holding on pretty tightly himself. "Mom got stuck with a bad bill at Shop 'N Go," he said.

"I got stuck too."

That day in the principal's office seemed like a hundred years ago. A lot had happened since. When Dad and I finally talked over what had happened he was still upset I'd put myself in danger, though he had to admit he was relieved to have the whole mess cleared up. Mom agreed. Then Mom and Dad agreed on something else. They let me get my ears pierced. I mean, why else would I be going without a ski cap in 20 degree weather, unless it was to show off my ears?

Things at St. Martin's were slowly improving. People had talked themselves out on the subject of Mr. Edmonds, counterfeiting, Dad, Lou Dargie, and women priests and had gotten back to church business as usual. Everyone except Mrs. Moorehead and Miss Kunzinger. They were the ones who had mailed out the anonymous letter to all the church members, just like I'd guessed. They had apologized, but now that Dad's new assistant, Florence Atkins, had come up with some way-out ideas, they were rallying their forces in protest. Dad had laughed and told Florence not to let it bother her. He was plenty busy himself, working with a new secretary now that Mrs. Cole had quit to take care of her kids full time.

Thinking about St. Martin's reminded me of what I had wanted to talk to Kenny about in the first place. We were more than halfway up the mountain, and if I were going to say it, I had better say it now.

"My dad is rector of St. Martin's. I guess you figured that out."

"Yeah."

"Well, I just wanted to say it's not as bad as people think, having a minister for a father. I mean, his job isn't the greatest, but it's what he likes, so I guess I'm stuck with it." The words weren't as hard to get out as I had thought. Practicing had helped.

"You're lucky."

"Huh?"

Kenny punched his ski gloves together as if he were cold and stared at the chair in front of us. "I said you're lucky your father is okay. Last month, the night after I saw you at the soccer game, my father was in a real bad car accident and he . . . he . . . got arrested for drunken driving. You must'a seen it in the paper."

I shook my head without being able to think of one intelligent thing to say.

Kenny was still studying the chair ahead of us. "It wasn't the first time. The judge ordered him to dry out . . . or go to jail. He's at the county halfway house now. I felt so lousy, I just couldn't face talking about it. . . ."

We were at the top of the lift. It was only my third trip up, and I hated the moment of re-entry. I swung the safety bar off my lap and tensed up, ready to slide off the chair. I made sure my ski tips were pointed up instead of down, like last time when I'd fallen on my face. I gripped my poles in my left hand, then pushed off with my right. There, my skis were on the ground. So were Kenny's, though he looked as awkward as I did. We both almost fell trying to get out of the way of the chairs behind us. We half-slid, half-hopped our way over to the Mary-Jane Trail, the easiest run on the mountain.

I was glad for the interruption. It gave me a chance to think about what Kenny had told me. He had really caught me by surprise. All this time Kenny had been so uptight about his own father, he hadn't cared one bit about Dad or his job.

"You didn't speak to me or have lunch with me ever since that day in Dunbridge because you were ashamed of your. . . ." I stopped myself just in time. "I mean, you didn't have anything to do with me because you thought I wouldn't want to have anything to do with you?" It came out all mixed up.

But Kenny knew what I meant. "Talking to you about it was easier than I figured." Kenny looked me right in the eye for the first time and smiled. "I guess that was my mistake."

"Yeah, I guess it was."

Kenny acted as relieved as I felt. As far as I was concerned, fathers were a closed subject on both sides. Kenny must have been thinking the same thing. He reached over and squeezed my arm. Even through my down jacket, his grip felt nice and strong the way I remembered.

"Coming on the right," someone shouted from behind.

We quickly sidestepped to let a whole bunch of kids go past us. They were laughing and talking as if skiing were easy. They didn't fool me. I knew how hard it was, and somehow that trail looked icier and even steeper than last time. I dug in my ski poles and arranged my skis in a snow plow position to make sure they wouldn't take off from under me.

"C'mon, I'll race you down. Loser buys winner a

Coke." Kenny challenged. He was all business as he pulled his goggles over his eyes and slipped his ski-pole handles on his wrists. Kenny must have caught on to skiing faster than I had. He looked really professional. Then I noticed his skis. They were in a snow plow position just like mine. I laughed.

"I'll race you," I agreed, "but only if we go down at the same time. Then we can pick each other up along the way."

Kenny followed my glance to our two pairs of snow-plowed skis. He had to laugh too, as we started slowly, cautiously, down the sloping mountain trail together.

ABOUT THE AUTHOR

Judith St. George received her Bachelor of Arts degree from Smith College in Northampton, Massachusetts. In her leisure time she enjoys sports, particularly tennis and paddle tennis.

Judith St. George is known for her ability to capture the spirit of a region. SHADOW OF THE SHAMAN was inspired by the years she and her family lived in the high desert country of eastern Oregon. THE SHAD ARE RUNNING is a story of Hudson River life in the 1830's. THE CHINESE PUZZLE OF SHAG ISLAND is a contemporary mystery that takes place on an island off the Maine coast, and THE GIRL WITH SPUNK is set against the first Woman's Rights Convention in Seneca Falls, New York.

Mrs. St. George currently lives with her family in Essex Fells, N. J. She and her husband, David have four teen-age children.